*Twenty years ago he'd disappeared
without a word, leaving her alone
on their wedding day . . .*

Now Will Combray has returned, older, but still hand-some and unpredictable, throwing Casey Becket's or-dered life into chaos. After his cruel and mysterious disappearance, Casey had turned to her best friend, Michael, the man who knew her as no one else.

Michael had promised to take care of Casey and give her a happy life, and he has kept his word. But now, with Will's sudden return, Casey must find the answer to an impossible question: What and who does she re-ally want? The wild, mercurial passion of Will? Or the comfortable, secure love of Michael?

Tugged in one direction by faithfulness and honor, and in another by pure desire, Casey must look back across the terrain of her life to discover which man will satisfy her heart.

"Grayson has a gift for capturing how relationships begin and develop and a sympathetically attuned insight into human nature."

Publishers Weekly

Also by Emily Grayson

THE OBSERVATORY
THE GAZEBO

EMILY GRAYSON

The FOUNTAIN

HarperTorch
An Imprint of HarperCollins*Publishers*

This is a work of fiction. Names, characters, places, and incidents are products of the author's imagination or are used fictitiously and are not to be construed as real. Any resemblance to actual events, locales, organizations, or persons, living or dead, is entirely coincidental.

HARPERTORCH
An Imprint of HarperCollins*Publishers*
10 East 53rd Street
New York, New York 10022-5299

Copyright © 2001 by Emily Grayson
ISBN: 0-06-103140-2

First HarperTorch paperback printing: July 2002
First William Morrow hardcover printing: August 2001

HarperCollins ®, HarperTorch™, and ❦™ are trademarks of Harper-Collins Publishers Inc.

Printed in the United States of America

Visit HarperTorch on the World Wide Web at www.harpercollins.com

10 9 8 7 6 5 4 3 2 1

For Susan Keating

The FOUNTAIN

Chapter
One

❧

❧ Two days before Casey Becket's twentieth wedding anniversary, her past came back to haunt her or, at the very least, astonish her. She wasn't prepared for such a visitation—no one ever is—but instead her thoughts were moving her only in the direction of Saturday, and the anniversary party that was to take place. She was sitting at the kitchen table, where she could often be found, her feet bare against the cool slate tiles, one foot tapping lightly to the percussive strains of jazz that were wafting from the CD player Michael had installed on a shelf above the spice rack. Before her on the table was a yellow legal pad covered with scrawled writing, all of it instructions she'd written to herself about things that had to be accomplished before the party. It was while Casey was going over the list and seeing what still needed to be done before Saturday that she saw a flash of movement out the back window, by the fountain.

Someone was there—one of the men from the party rental company, maybe. He was standing by the fountain, staring down into it, as if studying it for signs of life. By Saturday the fountain would be running again, bursts of water shooting upward, a fine mist falling on all the people who gathered in the yard. But now it was completely dry, still clotted with leaves and blossoms that had dropped from the trees that arched overhead. In recent years, and for no particular reason except perhaps the chaos of daily life, Casey and Michael had let it fall into disrepair. She supposed now that perhaps it had become a bit of an eyesore, but not so much that it should be an object of fascination for a stranger. And then the man looked up from the fountain, to the house, to the window where Casey Becket sat at a table, staring back at him.

The Fountain

๛

Her hand flew involuntarily to her mouth, as if some primitive part of her had recognized him before she could even realize what, or whom, she was seeing. And then there was no mistaking it: Some twenty-odd years after he had disappeared from her life, Will Combray had suddenly walked back into it.

She stood up shakily at the table and silently commanded herself to get a grip. For a "grip," whatever that was, really, was what she needed now more than anything. For a moment she and Will looked at each other through the screened window, neither of them saying a word. It was difficult, in this first, adrenalized moment of shocked recognition, to tell the difference between what she was really seeing and what her memory wanted her to see. But even at this distance, even staring through the screen, Casey could identify one thing that hadn't changed at all over the years: Will's smile. It was an expression that she immediately recognized as his, a slight upturn of one side of the lips, as though he'd recently had a shot of novocaine. A sleepy, slow smile, the kind that men might barely notice but that women always loved.

"Hello, Vanilla," he said.

It was a nickname from so long ago, and the sound of it now sent a peculiar sensation unraveling through her. The familiar word, in that familiar voice—it was almost as though no time had passed at all. And then Casey realized that she had always known it would be like this when Will returned. Not *if. When.* For as shocking as it was to look out the back window one morning and see the man she'd loved so long ago suddenly appear, it wasn't really surprising. It was, in a way, inevitable. It was as if she'd known all along that Will would one day come back, and that he would do it as he'd left: unexpectedly.

She walked to the kitchen door and threw it open, stepping out into the yard. "It *is* you," she said, and then the two of them just stood there, staring at each other across the lawn as if in a silent endurance contest, neither of them daring to speak or move any closer. There would be no running, no hugging, no open arms and cascading tears of happiness; this was not the kind of reunion that called for the usual displays of unfettered emotion. Instead, Casey and Will just looked and looked, absorbing what they saw, each appraising how the other had changed and somehow not changed, the overlay of age upon youth, like layers of paint spread on a canvas.

Will Combray and Casey Becket were now a grown man and woman. The last time they had been together, they were teenagers. Their faces had been narrower then, more defined. Both of them had had long, wild hair back then, too. Will was still unmistakably handsome, if slightly thicker featured, his sand-colored hair threaded with silver. He had once been an eighteen-year-old in a flannel shirt and jeans and scuffed Frye boots, who had occupied all her thoughts, and here he was now, a forty-year-old man in an expensive-looking white cotton shirt and loosened silk tie, probably well off and apparently tired. He walked closer then, and she noticed that he had a scar on his chin, something that hadn't been there the last time she'd seen him. He'd had a life without her, a life that included other people, and other places, and even a small scar that cut a raised diagonal across his chin, giving him the slightly raffish appearance of a pirate. A pirate executive, she thought giddily.

As for herself, Casey knew she came across as a

delicately pretty woman, someone who seemed still youthful and appealing and slightly arty, though perhaps lacking the concentrated girlish beauty she'd once had. For a moment, she felt as if she might cry, though whether for the eighteen-year-old Will had once been, or for the eighteen-year-old she'd once been, or simply from the exhaustion of the startling moment, she couldn't say.

"I hope I didn't scare you," Will said. And then, in a quieter voice, he added, "You know, you look exactly the way I imagined."

Casey smiled but didn't answer him. There was something tentative in Will's manner that was unfamiliar to her, even perplexing. Once, he'd been brazen, sure of himself in the way only an eighteen-year-old can be—though, she supposed, it was a brazen act to have come here after all these years, and especially after what he'd done to her.

"I guess you want to come in," Casey said after a moment.

"Yes," he said. "If that's okay."

She nodded, though really she had no idea. *Was* it okay? Maybe it was the worst idea in the world; it was impossible to tell. But Casey had no time to think this through, to be rational about the situation, to try to figure out what it might mean that after all these years Will Combray suddenly wanted to see her again, so instead she simply opened the door and let the first man she had ever loved into her house.

They sat together in the kitchen, drinking ice water from tall blue glasses. The kitchen was a place where Casey Becket often spent a good part of her afternoon, not because her culinary skills were particularly extensive but simply because it was by far the best room in the house, filled with light and plants and an outsize oval maple table that Michael had built when they were first married. "It's because I want there to be lots of people around it," Michael had said when she'd delicately commented on how incredibly large the table was. "Children, and friends, and family," he'd told her. "The whole nine yards." He'd gotten his wish, for the table was almost always populated. Long meals had often been spent here, with plenty of food and wine for the adults, and juice and milk poured from plastic jugs for the kids, and music drifting in from the speakers, and everybody always comfortable.

Somehow, though, she doubted that Michael had ever imagined Will Combray one day sitting at this table. It seemed like a betrayal, in fact, for Casey to have even invited him to sit here. But really, she asked herself, what was wrong with it? They were just a man and a woman sitting together, drinking ice water.

Will swallowed almost an entire glass of water at once and then asked for a refill, which she stood and got for him. Had he been running? Casey wondered. Had he not drunk anything in days? He had a parched quality to him that was puzzling, though maybe, she thought, it came from nerves. *Nerves.* Casey hadn't ever known that Will Combray possessed them. She was waiting for him to explain himself, to tell her how he had wound up here in Longwood Falls, of all places, so many years after he'd gone away for good. But it seemed as if he was planning to take his time. And of course she would let him, though some part of her wanted to yank him by his collar and shake him, shouting harshly in his

face, "What in God's name do you think you're doing here?"

But she would act cool; it gave her more dignity,
even if it was just posturing. Besides, Casey thought,
Will was the one who ought to feel vulnerable here,
not her. She was surrounded in this room by the
things of her life, and from the evidence it would
have been obvious to just about anyone sitting here
that Casey Becket's life was full and worthwhile. On
the walls of the kitchen were the framed pictures of
herself with Michael and their children: the twins,
Rachel and Hannah, who were going to be sopho-
mores at Cornell, and eighteen-year-old Alex, who
had just graduated from high school and would be a
freshman in the fall at his father's alma mater, the
Rhode Island School of Design.

Also on the walls were the rows of framed certifi-
cates that honored Casey, again and again, as
Teacher of the Year at Longwood Falls Primary
School. There were pictures of her and her students,
the kids all crowded excitedly around this energetic,
pretty, playful teacher they adored. Her students often stayed in touch after they left her class, coming
back for visits, sending her postcards and small

presents even years later, telling her how much she had meant to them and how she had forever shaped their lives. Will would only have to look around him and take note of all this indisputable evidence of the richness of her life, and the warmth and serenity of the room, and he would have no choice—he couldn't possibly miss it: Casey had been not only fine without him but better than fine.

"You've turned this room into such a beautiful place," Will said suddenly, as if on cue. "It's so warm and inviting now. Almost like a den instead of a kitchen."

"Thank you," Casey said. "We spend a lot of time sitting in here. I guess you can probably tell."

"And your family," he said, nodding in the direction of a cluster of photographs. "Very impressive, too. Your son there," he went on, pointing to a graduation picture.

"Alex," she said.

"Alex. He has his mother's eyes," said Will.

"Yes, everybody says that," Casey replied, as if to make sure Will didn't get it into his head to consider that his opinions were particularly original or special. There was silence for a moment. "So," she said. "How about you and *your* life?"

He laughed—a brief, sour laugh, she thought—and then he said, "I should have brought my résumé. That would make it easier to fill you in on everything." He took a breath. "I live in San Francisco, in a modern house overlooking the bay. I've done well," he said simply. Then he paused for a moment, as if what he was about to say next was hard for him. "As far as my personal life goes," Will continued, "I have to admit it's been less than stellar. Like you, I got married. Twice. I've had two wives, both of them gone now. One of them very recently."

"Gone?" she said. "Do you mean they died?"

He shook his head. "Gone to divorce court," he said. "I didn't really know how to be married, I guess. And as far as children go, no, I never had any. By the time either of my wives and I reached a point in our marriage at which we might consider having a family, we were busy considering whether we ought to stay married. And the answer, both times, was no."

Casey felt sympathetic toward him, but she

couldn't say she was surprised by what he'd told her. Will wasn't the marrying kind; that had once been made very clear to her. But something about seeing him as the divorcing kind made it even worse, as though he'd been trying throughout his adult life to fit into the world, to find a place of comfort, like a dog turning round and round in his little dog bed in order to settle in for the night. Apparently, Will had never found that comfortable position. A man didn't travel back into his past in order to convey how well everything had worked out, but he might come back, she knew, because he had unfinished business.

Will was playing with his glass now, one long finger ringing the rim, tracing a circle over and over again. He certainly had to know that if he came here, back into this house where he had been so long ago, it wouldn't be seen by Casey simply as a benign, sentimental act. He'd be stirring up something that had been left untouched all these years. Was the past stirrable? Casey wondered. As Will sat across from her in the kitchen, she found her thoughts coming loose, painting unbidden images in her mind. And one of those images was of Will—this Will, fully grown Will—uncurling his hand from the glass and reaching across the table to touch her neck. His hand on her neck, in this image, was cold and slightly damp from the ice water that had been in the glass.

Casey blinked, once; yes, all right, so Will Combray could still excite her after all these years. That didn't prove anything. "Will," she suddenly said, her voice thinner and more strained. "What is it you want from me?" It was as though she couldn't stand the wait any longer, couldn't play this game called "Now we are forty and oh so civil." It was one thing to sit here with him and chat all about Michael and the children, and tell him how her marriage had lasted, and feel vaguely superior about that fact. But it was quite another to get to the truth—and to get to it swiftly.

He nodded. "It's a fair question," he said. "But it's hard to answer. I don't know what I want from you, exactly. I could tell you I was here to apologize, but I know those would be meaningless words, and much too late, I'm afraid." He glanced up from the glass to Casey, then back down. "I'm here, I suppose," he went on, "because I'm lost."

Lost. It wasn't the word she'd expected. Casey hadn't known what to expect, but "lost" wasn't it.

She shook her head, letting him know she didn't have the faintest idea of what he meant or what he wanted her to understand. Will shook his head, too, as if he didn't know what he meant, either. And then he nodded, as if, suddenly, he did know.

"My wife left me," he said. "Walked out on me last Friday. I came home from work, and she was sitting in the living room with her luggage packed. She's already hired a lawyer, and she told me I should find one, too."

"I'm very sorry," Casey said quietly.

"Of course, I'd been through this once before, but even so, it's hit me hard," said Will. "When my first wife left, I told myself that it was her, not me. That she was the one who couldn't be pinned down, couldn't get accustomed to domestic life. After all, she was a bit of a free spirit; she liked to stay out late, travel all over creation. It took me a long time, but I did recover. But my second wife, Julie, she was completely different. Liked to stay home. Liked to be with me, I thought. And yet, finally, she told me it wasn't working." Will turned away from Casey slightly, his gaze wandering to the yard, and out to the fountain. "I don't know how to make things

work, Casey," he said softly. "I guess I never have."
Then he shrugged. "After Julie left the other day,
and the house was empty, I started walking through
all the rooms, thinking about everything that's happened to me. And I began to ask myself: When did
everything start to fall apart? Of course, I knew the
answer to that one right away." He looked directly at
her, then said, "It fell apart the moment I left you."

Casey could only look back at him, questioningly,
startled.

"And I'm not sure what it is I want from you," he
went on. "I don't think I really want anything at all,
except to see you and to say this to you in person. So
here I am. Lost, like I told you."

"And I'm supposed to 'find' you or something?"
Casey said.

"No," Will said emphatically. "No, no. Not at all. I
don't expect anything from you, Casey. No favors,
certainly. I guess I just needed to go back to the place
where it all began to unravel. Where it all started to
not 'work.' To see you again and hope it would
spark something in me, some recognition of why
things have turned out the way they have. Badly, I
guess you could say, at least as far as my emotional

life is concerned. And, I don't know, maybe to figure out a way to get . . . back. Back to who I was once, or to what I wanted out of life, or *something*."

As she listened to him, she realized how rapidly her heart was beating, like a small, nervous animal's, and how surreal this moment had become. Here he was, the man she had thought about from time to time over the years, the memories returning every few months out of nowhere—when she saw a young couple in love downtown, perhaps, or when one of her daughters brought a boyfriend home. Sometimes she dreamed of Will, too, and she would wake up next to Michael feeling confused and slightly embarrassed, for the dreams were usually somewhat erotic. And if Michael ever woke up then and asked her what was going on, she would answer, "Nothing," because nothing was when it came to Casey Becket and Will Combray.

When Casey Becket was eighteen years old and went by the name Casey Stowe, she had fallen in love with Will Combray. Desperately, gaspingly in love, as though they'd invented the entire concept. So much in love that it had taken up all her energy and all her thoughts. She couldn't have a conversation with anyone or actually sit still long enough to read a book all the way through. She dropped things; a fork went clanging to the linoleum during dinner, a hairbrush flew out of her hand when she stood before her mirror getting ready for bed. This was what love did, Casey knew: It unhinged you.

But she was forty now, and unhinging was no longer an option. Gasping, desperate love was something you fell in when you were young, and then when you looked back on it later, when you were older, you could only shake your head and marvel at how young you were once. Or, at least, that's what she'd always done, in the twenty-plus years since she'd last experienced that kind of love.

"So tell me," she asked Will now, because she wanted to know. "Seeing me again, has it sparked something in you?"

"Oh, yes," he said. "It has."

And then he slowly, purposefully stood up and walked around the table, coming over by her chair. She felt herself take in a hard, uneasy breath. This was wrong, she knew, and yet she could only acknowledge it but not stop it. She was sitting and he was standing, hovering above her and looking down, and then he crouched beside her chair so that they were on the same level. Their faces were suddenly close, too close for this still to be a normal catching-up conversation between two people who hadn't seen each other in a long time. And yet she didn't pull away from him abruptly; she didn't stand up and move back from him. Something kept her fastened into that chair, as though it were a car on a roller coaster, and an invisible safety bar held her braced for the ride.

And then she knew with certainty that there *would* be a ride. And it was beginning right now.

"Casey," Will said softly, "you seem incredibly nervous."

"Well, I am," she said.

"Should I go away?" he asked.

She didn't say anything. His face was even closer, and then suddenly it was against hers, and Will was pressing his mouth not to her mouth but to her cheek—chaste and yet not chaste at all.

He drew away after a couple of seconds, and both of them were flushed and somehow slightly changed by this strange moment.

"What should we do?" he asked her quietly.

"I don't know," she said, still locked in place in her chair.

They stayed like that for a few more seconds, neither of them speaking, and then finally Will sighed and stood up. "I think, actually, I *should* go," he said.

"All right," she said.

"For now, anyway."

"All right," she said again.

"I'm staying at the Longwood Falls Inn," Will said, in a voice that tried hard to sound casual. "I have to fly back to San Francisco on Saturday. If by any chance you feel like continuing this conversation, I'm in Suite 206." He paused at the back door, staring out at the yard and the fountain, and then he added quietly, "I'll leave it entirely up to you."

At dinner that night, sitting around the large maple table with her family, fragrant plates of pasta primavera steaming before them, Casey tried to bring herself to tell Michael that Will had visited her today after all this time, but she found herself unable to. It wasn't that Alex was sitting at the table, too, for even with her teenage son there, she might easily have said to Michael, "You'll never guess who came to the house today." Alex knew nothing about his mother's old relationship with Will and probably never would. She hoped, in a way, that she would be able to mention Will's visit casually to Michael, for that would have taken some of the electrical charge out of it, normalizing it, making it more ordinary than she really felt it to be. But that would have been false; she'd only be playacting, putting on a cheerful voice to describe events that were, somehow, anything but.

And so she said nothing. Instead, she deflected questions about her day at home and asked Alex about his day at The Scoop, the overpriced ice cream shop with its designer flavors (Caramel Apple, French Toast with Syrup) where he had a summer job to earn extra money for college in the fall. Alex often amused his parents with stories from The Scoop, a place that was apparently filled with more drama than might be expected. Alex was a good listener, and he often picked up small details from people's lives: whose marriage was breaking up over the course of a hot fudge sundae ("Should have been a banana split," Michael commented), who had been given bad news at the doctor's.

∽

"Things were pretty quiet," Alex said today. "I guess lots of people are away on vacation now."

"Or else," said Michael, "they're at home primping and preening, starting to get ready for our anniversary party."

"Yeah, Dad," said Alex, "I'm sure that must be it. No one in town can think about anything else but you and Mom and your special day. Everyone's obsessed."

Michael smiled at his son, then turned to Casey. "How was your day, Case?" he asked. "Were things livelier around here than at The Scoop?"

"No, sorry," she said in a small voice. "Nothing particularly juicy to report, I'm afraid."

There was simply no point in telling him that Will had been there. What had happened between the teenage versions of Will and Casey had taken place before she and Michael were married, and it certainly couldn't affect anything now. She didn't even know Will Combray anymore. Of course, choosing not to tell Michael about Will's visit was in itself suspicious, at least to her. She played with the edges of her paper napkin as she sat at the table, fraying them into fringe.

ॐ

"Actually, I worked on the final touches for the party," she told Michael, which was true: After Will had let himself out the back door, she'd somehow forced herself to sit down at the table again and get a few items crossed off her list.

"Good," said Michael. "You know, I'm really starting to look forward to Saturday. I mean, I've been looking forward to it all along, of course, but now it's in a new way. This is going to be a terrific party."

Saturday. Casey's first thought, disturbingly, improbably, was that Saturday was the day Will was going back to San Francisco.

"It's close enough now that I can't really think about much of anything else," Michael went on. "All day at the studio, I kept picturing all the people arriving, the tents up, the band playing, the fountain going full blast—"

"The *presents*," said Alex, drawing out the word in a parody of greed.

"Nope," said Michael. "The invitations clearly said 'No gifts, please.' "

"Oh, right, that'll stop people," said Alex.

"We're not doing it for the presents," said Michael with mock exasperation. "We're doing it for—"

"Love," Alex interrupted.

"You're hopeless, kiddo," Michael said, laughing. "But you'll understand one day. Maybe. If you're lucky, and find someone who'll put up with you."

This back-and-forth between father and son was the kind of banter that Casey usually enjoyed watching during dinner. So why, tonight, did she wish she was somewhere else, somewhere far away from the land of husbands and children and the reassuring, murmuring comforts of family life?

She knew why. It wasn't Michael. He was a splendid husband and father by anyone's reckoning, including her own—a tall, dark-haired, shy man who had taken his artist's imagination and his skilled hands and built from scratch a successful business—Becket Woodworks, a furniture studio with commissions lined up for at least the next two years. Michael was indisputably a loving husband, a tender and funny father. No, it wasn't him; it couldn't be him.

It was her.

Just a week earlier, Casey had been looking forward to the party, yet now, suddenly, it seemed to her somehow *wrong*. It had been Michael's idea; he was more nostalgic about anniversaries than she was. But Casey had eagerly gone along with it, and so had the kids. The twins would be coming home tomorrow from their college town in order to attend. And despite his kidding around at the table tonight, Casey knew that Alex was excited, too, because she and Michael had let him invite some of his friends from school, including his girlfriend, Amy, a star junior-varsity softball player with long legs and silky red hair. Casey loved throwing huge parties in the yard, because they reminded her of the parties her own beloved parents had once thrown in this yard, and the ones that Michael's parents had thrown in the same yard, and then the ones that she and Michael had thrown, after they were married. And on Saturday they would stand by the newly vigorous fountain in the middle of the yard and renew their vows.

But the fact was, Casey was suddenly in no mood to celebrate her marriage. This was a disquieting thought, and she couldn't defend it even to herself. But from her place in the center of this family, Casey

Becket felt herself lift up above everyone and hover there at a distance, watching everything like the Cheshire cat. Unlike the Cheshire cat, however, she wasn't smiling. It was as though she was no longer a participant in her own family but merely an observer, and all because of Will's visit—all because she now had a secret she'd never asked for, and a burden.

"Hey, are you all right?" she heard Michael asking, his voice sounding muffled and far away.

"Yes," she said, blinking and inwardly trying to find a way to return to him. *Earth to Casey*, Michael used to say to her when they were kids and Casey started to daydream. *Earth to Casey. Do you read me, Casey?* Back then, of course, it was a lot easier to return to the room, to the conversation. But now Casey had to force herself to stay focused on what was before her: her husband, her son, the party this weekend, instead of on the man—the lost man—who, even as she sat with her family, might be lying on his back in a bed at the Longwood Falls Inn, his arms folded across his chest, thinking only of her.

Chapter
Two

꒰ Long before Will Combray came along, Michael was there. Always, there had been Michael. And if Casey felt as though she'd known him forever, it was only because she had.

On February 24, 1958, a handmade sign hung on the front door of 9 Strawberry Street: WELCOME, MICHAEL LEWIS BECKET, 8 LBS., 2 OZ.!! Hardly two months later, on April 18, right next door, another sign read, WELCOME, CASEY MORGAN STOWE, 6 LBS., 3 OZ.!! Late at night during the warm months of that first year, one or another of the Becket or Stowe parents could often be found outside in the backyard at night, walking a baby around so he or she would finally get to sleep. They developed a running joke during those weary walks: Sometimes the parent from one family would sense the presence of the parent from the other family through the hedge and call out, "Who goes there?" Then they'd get together and stroll the yards side by side, chatting quietly or even singing an impromptu, off-key duet, until both babies finally lost the fight against sleep.

It was a good time, those early days: a time of talcum powder and hectic meals on the fly and a sense that men and women were created to raise babies, for what else in life offered such wholehearted if exhausting pleasure? It was a satisfaction that arose not just from the moment but from all that was to come. Eleanor Stowe and Janice Becket often talked about how the babies would grow into good friends as they got older, and how gratifying that would be to watch.

But the babies, as babies do, had minds of their own. As they turned into children, no friendship was forged between them. Michael appeared indifferent to Casey; instead, he remained preoccupied with the little projects he was always starting.

The Fountain

᠅

Things, to four-year-old Michael Becket, were vastly more interesting than people. He was a dark-eyed, serious little boy who liked putting things together, though not as much as he liked taking them apart, if only so he could immediately set about putting them together again. All he needed to get him through a rainy day was a broken alarm clock or a ruptured toaster. When Casey, fair-haired and sensitive, came over to see him, he could usually be found in the middle of his family's linoleum kitchen floor, surrounded by sprockets and gears.

"Can I help?" she would ask after a while, and he would look up at her and scowl briefly.

"Don't need help," he would say, returning to his work.

This went on—and on and on and on, as far as the parents of the two children were concerned—until one day, out of the blue, Michael finally agreed that Casey could assist with the robot he was building out of Dole pineapple cans. And from that day forward, according to family legend, the children were inseparable, a fact that their mothers—and, eventually, even their fathers—loved to dwell on.

"It's as though," Tom Becket said to his wife one

night, watching the children play under the Beckets' kitchen table, "they're a miniature married couple."

And it was true. The children had finally become a unit, a solid twosome who loved each other protectively, modeling their behavior into some version of the way their mothers and fathers loved each other in the early 1960s. It was a peaceful time in the yards and homes of Longwood Falls back then, and summer weekends often included barbecues on the hibachi grill that Warren Stowe had recently purchased. The adults ate thick steaks striped with A-1 Sauce, while the children wolfed down hot dogs before returning to their endless games.

It was during one of these backyard suppers in August of 1965 that Tom Becket had an idea. "Well, here's a thought," he said after the meal, as his wife lit a citronella candle to keep the mosquitoes at bay and Warren poured another batch of foamy daiquiris from the glass container of the Waring blender. The evening was warm and calm. Somewhere in the distance, a lawn mower buzzed. "You know what we could do?" Tom went on. "Get rid of the hedge that separates the houses."

"Just like that?" asked Warren. "Just get rid of it?

ॐ

That's a fairly revolutionary idea, coming from you, Tom."

"Well, maybe you're right," said Tom, slumping slightly back into his lawn chair.

"No, no, it's good," came the chorus before him. "Let's do it!" said Eleanor Stowe above the crowd, and then from Tom's own wife, Janice, rose the decisive vote, softly, as if she were still warming to the idea even as she pushed the sentiment over the top: "Yes. Why not? Yes!"

"But what about privacy?" said Warren Stowe. "What about individual families having their own secrets?"

"Oh, God, give it up," said his wife. "We don't have any secrets. I wish we *did*," she added.

"It's true," said Janice. "We don't have any secrets, either. Nothing serious, anyway. Nothing we'd need a *hedge* to hide, God knows."

All four adults laughed at their own innocence and at the realization that none of them had a dark side of any consequence. So why not live less like neighbors and more like family? So what if it wasn't the usual small-town thing to do? In the mugginess of an idle August evening on Strawberry Street, and perhaps inspired as much by the alcohol content of the daiquiris as by the genuine affection they felt for each other, the two couples agreed to tear down the hedge that separated their two homes and create one big backyard.

Within days, the men had chopped away the shrubbery that divided the property into two equal lots. But then, with the hedge gone, the lawn looked oddly naked and exposed. So Tom had another idea: Because he was a plumber, he said, he would build a fountain where the hedge had stood. It would straddle the property line, standing in honor of the solidarity of the families and displaying two stone angels in its center, one to represent Casey as a baby, the other to represent baby Michael. Tom had his co-workers help him install the delicate but substantial stone fountain, and then, one memorable evening, he called the two families together while he ran to the side of his house to turn on the spigot. "Here goes nothing," he called, and suddenly a great gust of water leaped high into the evening air, baptizing the baby angels of stone—and the ones of flesh and blood, too, as Casey and Michael ran celebratory circles around and around the fountain, dancing in the mist that landed on both the Beckets' property and the Stowes'. The adults couldn't help themselves: They clapped, and then they, too, danced a little— the Watusi, the Swim. If the hedge had been too much for the adjoining backyards and the absence of the hedge too little, then the fountain was somehow Goldilocks-perfect: *Just right.*

And so the enchanted, fairy-tale bond that had been sealed in daiquiris and humidity now assumed a more substantial form. The two households continued to behave like one extended family; there was almost nothing to separate them anymore. The mothers were best friends, the fathers were best friends, and—there they were, chasing each other around the backyard every morning, circling the fountain in their swimsuits, and then in their corduroy-and-suspenders autumn outfits, and finally in their fleece-trimmed and mitten-clipped midwinter mammothness—the children were best friends, too.

"Just look at them," Janice said with a sigh late one afternoon, while she and the other adults sat in the Stowe kitchen sipping hot chocolate and watching the children spacewalk through the snowdrifts.

"You know," she went on, "I wouldn't be surprised if they married each other one day."

Janice was, in fact, voicing precisely what every other parent in the room had been thinking at that moment, and the silence that followed her offhand remark was almost unbearable. Casey and Michael were like two little grown-ups, looking out for each other, traversing the big, barren world together. What could possibly be more satisfying for any of the mothers or fathers in the kitchen that afternoon than if their children were to fall in love with each other one day . . . maybe marry . . . and—who knows?—become a mother and a father themselves?

"Well, kids today," Eleanor finally responded. "They're so much more independent than we ever were." Then, after a moment, she added, "But you never know."

"No, you never do know," said her husband. "There's no telling what might happen." Warren blew lightly on his mug of hot chocolate, then said, "But it would be something, wouldn't it?"

And then Tom Becket spoke up. "It would be something, that's for sure," he said. "But we've got to be careful. What would make us happy might not be what's best for them. I wouldn't want to push them into anything. Let them be who they are; let them find what they want in the long run without having to be influenced by what *we* want for them. I mean, that's the point of all this, right?" And he gestured then, around the kitchen, toward the yard, somehow suggesting the whole of the lives that the Beckets and the Stowes had established for themselves, side by side, in the town of Longwood Falls, New York. "That's what we're doing all this for, so that our children can have their own lives."

"Of course, of course," the others agreed with slight wistfulness, because they knew that Tom Becket, as usual, was right. The two sets of parents who had gathered around the kitchen table in the fading afternoon light belonged to a generation that had never been given enough time to really find out what they wanted in life. When they had come of age, marriage and parenthood were prerequisites for adulthood, and these they had accomplished early, 1950s style. The men had hastily decided on careers—plumbing for Tom, accounting for Warren—based on practicality, not passion. First and foremost, they were husbands and fathers; the women, wives and mothers. The men were providers, the women protectors. The two marriages were strong and loving and secure, and the roles that each of them had accepted within those marriages were sound and rewarding. They wouldn't change a thing for themselves; there was no question of that. But the four of them also sensed that maybe, just maybe, there might be something more for their children—more choices, more time to make those choices, more . . . *everything*. Why not? That was the point, wasn't it? That was the opportunity—the unspoken, unacknowledged, but unmistakable legacy—that they wanted to pass on to their children: more.

By the time Michael Becket and Casey Stowe reached high school in the mid-1970s, they were famous in their town. Or, rather, their relationship was famous, for no other boy and girl seemed capable of remaining so close while still keeping things at the simple level of friendship. All around them, boys and girls were doing what boys and girls have always done—not just fall in love but fall in love as if their generation were the one that discovered love. In this case, the boys and girls dressed in almost identical jeans and plaid flannel shirts, the boys' hair as long as the girls'; they held hands as they strolled the gleaming school hallways, stopping at every corner in order to kiss frantically, if fumblingly, letting the world know they were in love because, now more than ever, love was nothing to hide—indeed, it was something to proclaim proudly, openly, triumphantly. Girls covered entire sheets in their school notebooks with doodles of boys' names in psychedelic marker colors, while boys sat in their parents' garages and composed moody songs on the electric guitar for their girlfriends. Everyone seemed to be swooning all at once, intoxicated by these new and overwhelming feelings.

Everyone, that is, except Michael and Casey. Michael had grown to be tall, dark-haired, and slender, with a hockey stick parked on his shoulder in the winter and a baseball bat slung loosely over that same shoulder in spring. Casey was small, golden, beautiful, and talented at the piano. They made a striking couple, or would have, if in fact they had been a couple in the usual sense. But instead they were best friends who, because they had known each other all their lives, understood each other better than anyone else did, and maybe better than a regular boyfriend or girlfriend ever could. Their relationship was special, they told themselves; their relationship was old-fashioned, said everyone else. Whatever it was, it was unique in the 1970s in the town of Longwood Falls.

"Why," Casey asked Michael one day after school, as the two of them sat on the swing by the pond with their geometry textbooks lying open and ignored in their laps, "does everyone think that what we do—or don't do—is so incredibly weird?"

"You know why," said Michael. "Because if it were them, they'd be jumping into each other's arms right this minute, saying, 'Oh, baby, baby, baby.'"

Casey laughed. "But not us," she said. "No 'baby, baby, baby' here."

"No, definitely not," Michael agreed. But he had a strange expression on his face then, and he looked away from her quickly.

"What is it?" she asked.

"Nothing," he said.

She was sure it wasn't nothing but chose not to press the point. Instead, she slapped her book shut and said, "Tell me a story."

And so he did. He knew what she meant. Sometimes Michael went along with his father on his plumbing rounds. Michael had told his father that he had no intention of joining the business, and to his surprise and relief, his father had agreed that a boy with Michael's significant technical skills could indeed find a more artistic and perhaps more personally rewarding outlet for working with his hands. Still, Tom Becket sometimes needed a helper, and Michael sometimes needed a little extra cash. Afterward, Casey always grilled Michael about what he'd witnessed in other people's houses.

"Don't you see, it's like a wonderful novel," she would say. "So give me all the details. Don't leave anything out. Tell me a story."

"Okay," he would begin. "Let's see. Oh, I know. The Guarnaccis?"

Casey would nod her head eagerly.

"Well, the strange thing with the Guarnaccis," Michael went on, "is that their house has almost no furniture in it at all."

"Really?" Casey said.

"Absolutely," Michael told her. "In the living room there's maybe a coffee table, that's all. And the kitchen—well, my dad and I were in there working on the sink, and I have to say I have no idea how they eat their meals, because they don't have chairs."

"Maybe they sit on the floor," said Casey, picturing Albert Guarnacci, a heavyset man with a potbelly, struggling to his feet after a meal on the floor. "Maybe they're secretly Japanese and they eat on mats."

One day Michael had seen an irate man slap his wife in the kitchen of a house on Birdsong Lane, and this had led to a talk with Casey about what a husband's responsibility to a wife was. "He should never be so disrespectful as to think that it's his role to teach her a lesson," Michael said. "The man and the woman have to be totally equal partners. No one should be in charge or think they're superior to the other. That's the kind of marriage I'm going to have someday."

"Mmm."

The two of them on this occasion had been talking in the backyard on Strawberry Street, drawn out of their houses and over to the fountain, as they often were, by the warm night air. Certainly Casey agreed with everything that Michael had said about the man and the woman in a marriage needing to be equal partners. The larger question for her was marriage itself. She looked at her parents' marriage and thought it was perfectly fine, for them; for herself, however, she wanted to find out what else was out there. What she knew of love and passion, she'd learned from TV and movies and books. What she wanted to know now, she could learn only from life.

That was part of the attraction of Michael's stories, she knew. She never discussed this with Michael. It was perhaps the only thing they never discussed, she reflected now, dipping one hand into the pooled water of the fountain. But the glimpses his stories gave her into the way other people in Longwood Falls lived their lives reinforced for her the feeling, the certainty, that there must be something else out there. Something *more*.

And there was. This, she knew for a fact. Twice a week, Casey was visited at the house by Dorian Bradley, an unmarried music teacher in her late twenties who lived three blocks away on Bancroft Road. Prior to moving here, Dorian had lived in New York City—in Greenwich Village, to be exact. More to the point, Dorian had really *lived*—perhaps lived too much, she'd confided to her favorite student— and so now she'd decided to spend a few years in a small, peaceful town in order to get her bearings.

"I tell you, Casey," Dorian would say after Casey had finished playing one of Satie's *Gymnopédies* to Dorian's satisfaction, "the real world is nothing like Longwood Falls. You're lucky to grow up here, where there's a calmness, a kindness to everything. When you get out there, you'll see what I mean. Your eyes will *pop*. Frankly, my early twenties exhausted me. The pace. The intensity. The men." She shuddered. "It's wonderful to have something all your own—a world that belongs only to you. But, finally, I needed a rest."

Dorian Bradley was unlike anyone else Casey had ever met; she was worldly and engaging and spoke her mind, and even though she was an adult, she instructed Casey to call her Dorian instead of Miss Bradley or, as some women nowadays wanted to be called, *Ms.* Bradley. She was beautiful, too, with dark henna-colored hair, high cheekbones, and a tall body that a fashion magazine might describe as "willowy." When Dorian came to the Stowes' house every Tuesday and Thursday afternoon, Casey's parents cleared out of the living room. Teacher and student settled side by side on the blond-wood

bench in front of the upright piano, working hard together, but it was what happened during the breaks
that made the lessons memorable for Casey: They
talked about the world. *Tell me everything you know*,
Casey wished she could ask, for it was clear that Dorian knew a great deal about many things beyond the
town lines of Longwood Falls. And during those moments, Casey felt that she was finding her true calling.
Not as a pianist, despite whatever genuine talent she
exhibited. As a teacher. Because this, Casey saw, was
what a good teacher like Dorian could do: instruct
you not just in the subject at hand, but also in *life*.

"What are you thinking about?" Michael asked
her now, by the fountain, and Casey realized that
she'd been silent for some time.

"My piano lessons," she said, truthfully if not altogether honestly.

"That's nice," Michael said. "I'm glad you have
the piano."

But something in his voice made Casey look up.
Michael, however, wasn't looking at her. Instead, he
was staring into the depths of the fountain's water.

"Casey," he said. "You and me, we really—" He
stopped himself in the middle of a sentence.

"What?" she asked.

"Nothing," he said. "Forget it."

"No, tell me. What is it?" She was reminded of the time on the swing by the town pond, when Michael had looked somehow miserable yet happy.

"This is hard for me—" he began now, and then his voice broke off and he turned away. His breathing seemed slightly labored. Casey could see his shoulders in the moonlight rising and falling, rising and falling. "Don't you get it?" he said suddenly, turning back to her.

His features had colored a little, darkening with something she hadn't seen in him before: embarrassment, was it? He'd never had a reason to be embarrassed in front of her, and she'd made sure never to give him one. He was always at ease with Casey in a way that people almost never were with each other, especially teenagers. But here, now, was a different Michael Becket, someone far from the casual, graceful next-door neighbor who could repair a stereo and catch a ball and braid strands of lanyard into an Indian bracelet to give to her without a trace of self-consciousness about the gesture.

That boy was gone, and in his place stood a serious, blushing teenager with an expression of anguish in his eyes.

He was attracted to her. Maybe he was even in love with her.

"Yes," she said finally, her voice tiny and unrecognizable. "I see."

"Do you?" he said. "Because I've got to know. It's driving me crazy. I know, I know, that's a cliché. But it's true. Clichés can be true, right? Because I really feel that I'm going to lose my mind if I can't find out. I can deal with the truth, one way or the other, I think. But I've got to know: Do you feel something for *me*? Or am I alone in this?"

Michael, alone? The idea almost made her laugh. He hadn't been alone as long as she'd known him, which was forever, and neither had she. Because they had each other. They'd *always* had each other. He was so much a part of her life, and she his, that she almost felt he *was* her, and she was sure he felt the same about her.

But now that was changed, and suddenly Casey didn't feel like laughing one bit. She realized that by broaching this subject, he had changed everything between them, shifting the balance so it could never

again be fully regained. Now they needed to know—
No, no, that wasn't right. Now *he* needed to know for
himself, and *she* needed to know for herself: Do we
merely love each other, or are we "in love"?

Suddenly she felt angry at Michael for having
done this, for having divided them this way. But she
couldn't stay angry, she realized just as suddenly,
because she also knew that it had been bound to
happen someday. All along, by saying how lucky
they were to have such a wonderful, platonic friendship, they were ignoring the truth. And the truth, as
she saw it now, was that there was in fact something
else between them. Casey felt it, realized that she
had felt it each time she saw his broad shoulders and
straight back when they went diving together every
summer, and when he dressed in a suit jacket to sing
in the chorus at school, and when he put on a ragged
old work shirt to help his father on a job and his
muscles were apparent—the elaborate, male ma-
chinery of them. Felt it, realized she felt it, and pre-
tended she didn't.

So now, standing by the fountain and assessing all
of this, reviewing the feelings that had been bub-

bling under the surface all this time, Casey decided she would be in love with Michael Becket.

"Is it okay?" he asked her. "Are you okay?"

She looked away for a moment in the moonlight, then nodded, almost unable to breathe. "I'm okay," she said. "I'm just . . . totally confused, that's all. This is very strange."

"I know," he whispered.

"I mean," she continued, "you're Michael, and you're suddenly *not* Michael. Do you know what I'm talking about?"

"I think I do," he said quietly. Then he stepped forward and gently, exploratorily, touched the edges of her hair, brushing them from her neck, all the while watching her expression, as if to ask, *Is this okay?* And it was okay, at least she thought it was, and her expression let him know that. He dipped his head down, like someone ducking as he walked beneath a low-slung chandelier, and then he kissed her.

Casey inhaled a hard breath, startled. Michael opened his mouth against hers, and the kiss lingered, somewhat inexpert but heartfelt. They were joining the throngs of teenagers at school who walked

✃

hand in hand and kissed by the lockers and the double doors of the cafeteria and anywhere else they could find. Michael's kiss tasted of him, was as tender and affectionate as he was. Casey could almost imagine how thrilled her parents and his would be if they happened to look out the windows of their side-by-side houses right now and saw what their children were doing.

But it didn't make her entirely happy to imagine such pleasure on her parents' part. She wanted something for herself, as Dorian Bradley had mentioned, something that wasn't just another part of the Becket-Stowe extended family of happiness. In a way, she thought, Michael had torn down the hedge that existed between the two of them, the dividing line that kept them separate.

"Michael," she said softly, after the kiss ended and they both stood there staring uncertainly at each other. "Let's not tell, okay?"

"Tell who?" he asked.

"Them. Our parents. About what's happened."

"Well, sure, fine," said Michael. He seemed to be thinking it over. "But I'm curious. Why not, Casey?" he asked. "Do you think they'll be upset or something? Because personally, I think it would be quite the opposite."

"Of course it would be quite the opposite," said Casey, slightly exasperated at his obtuseness on the subject. "And that's why I don't want them to know. Let's keep it private."

"Fine," he said, but he was still studying her face for reactions, trying to see what he ought to be doing now, how he ought to be behaving. The kiss, which was nice enough, had obviously changed everything, but in what way?

Casey was asking herself the same question. It wasn't as though they now had to get married to each other; it was the 1970s, after all, and this was only a kiss. Certainly Casey Stowe would kiss other people before she found one person to spend the rest of her life with.

But this wasn't about the rest of her life; it was about the rest of her summer, which, it was now clear, was going to be spent in a kind of furtive haze, at times exciting in its secrecy, at other times overwhelming.

The first kiss soon progressed into a series of touches and caresses, and within a few weeks

Michael and Casey became lovers. It wasn't something they discussed beforehand; it just happened one afternoon, while they were alone in a deserted patch of forest down by the reservoir, on a blue-and-yellow-striped picnic blanket that belonged to her parents, and which had, in its previous life, been only a surface on which to place a hamper that Eleanor Stowe had packed with chicken sandwiches, butterscotch brownies, and thermoses of lemonade. Now Casey and Michael were kissing and touching on that blanket, and Michael hovered above her, looking down. She could see the sky beyond his head, the clouds hurrying past in long white trails, and she thought of how enormous the world was but how well she and Michael, two people among billions, knew each other. They anchored each other in the earth; they made each other feel safe.

"I love you so much," he said to her then.

"I love you so much, too," she answered, and she realized they were both tacitly assenting to make love in a moment. They each knew they could trust the other, and that no matter what happened afterward, this lovemaking would never be something they would regret. And so they went forward with it. She closed her eyes, he moved himself against her, and she held him tightly.

They continued to meet in the same places they always had: the swing by the pond, the front porch of either one's house, the fountain in the joined backyard, the spot by the reservoir. And though Casey and Michael were never physical with each other out in the open, both sets of parents began to see a change in their children.

"It's happening, I think," Eleanor Stowe whispered to Janice Becket on the telephone one night.

Casey was walking past her parents' bedroom during this conversation and happened to catch these words, which, for a fleeting moment, she didn't associate with herself. Then, sickeningly, she did. Casey stopped in the hall and flattened herself against the wall to listen.

"The children, I mean," she heard her mother say. "They seem to be falling in love, Janice. It's so wonderful, I can hardly believe it. We've dreamed of it over the years, haven't we, and now here it is, as natural as anything. I'm so glad we never pushed them, never talked about it with them, or else they never would have found it out for themselves."

༚

There was a pause, as Eleanor Stowe listened to what Janice Becket had to say. "Oh, yes, yes, I agree, Janice. It's so . . . comfortable, isn't it? I guess the children have inherited our desire to have things seem to fit, you know?" She laughed a little. "Oh, I would be perfectly happy to throw them a wedding here in the backyard," she went on. "No, no, no, I know, of course, young people sometimes live together these days before getting married—not that I particularly approve of that, but it isn't my place to offer an opinion. But when they're older— mid-twenties, say—and if they want to marry, they can take their vows by the fountain. It would be the most wonderful day ever." She paused again. "I know they're trying to hide it from us," Eleanor said on the telephone, "but they haven't done a very good job, have they? Well, it doesn't matter. What matters is that everyone is so happy."

But out in the hallway at that moment, standing with her palms pressed against the wallpaper, not daring to move, Casey Stowe felt more unhappy than she'd ever been in her life.

Chapter
Three

꙰

～ When she looked out her bedroom window on the evening of Will's return, Casey saw a young man and a young woman sitting together in the moonlight on the edge of the fountain, and for one disoriented moment, she thought she was already asleep and dreaming of herself and Will when they were young. Then, returning quickly to reality, she realized that it was only her son, Alex, and his girlfriend, Amy. They were sitting with their heads close, and he was whispering something into her ear, making her laugh. Casey was awake, but in a way, she thought, dropping to the pillow, it was a dream: the way that more than twenty years can sweep past and you can suddenly find yourself transformed from an eighteen-year-old falling in love into a forty-year-old with a nearly grown son, himself now falling in love.

It was almost too much, the way time worked. In a couple of weeks, her son would be off to college. The loss of her daughters to college life had been wrenching enough. She still sometimes found herself pausing in the hall outside their bedroom door, wondering for a moment why they were so quiet in there, before realizing that of course they weren't there, they were at college. Alex, however, was the final child; after he left home, the quiet that Casey would encounter from time to time in this house would be coming not only from his room but from *everywhere*.

Still, it wasn't just to college that Casey was losing her son. It was to Amy, and to all the Amys in Alex's future. It was to adulthood. Already Alex was leaving, as if with every dip of his head toward Amy's ear and neck, he turned his back a little bit more on the house and parents he'd known forever. Which was as it should be, Casey knew, but that didn't make it easier. She realized suddenly that long ago when she was falling in love with Will Combray, this is what it must have been like for her parents. This, and worse.

Will was three miles away right this moment, probably just getting to bed in his suite at the Longwood Falls Inn. And because of this, Casey had trouble falling asleep. She just lay there, mentally checking on the thousand details she needed to attend to in the two days before the party. Tomorrow afternoon, the tent men would arrive, and so would the men with the folding chairs and the round tables, rolling them across the lawn to set them up. Tomorrow night, Hannah and Rachel would be arriving home from their college town, where they both had summer jobs, and then the following afternoon would be the party. Around and around Casey's mind raced, but where it stopped, again and again, was Suite 206.

How could she possibly concentrate on anything else? Will was there, so nearby, and it was up to her whether or not to see him. He needed her; it was a ridiculous notion, but there it was. She who'd once needed him as she had never needed anything or anybody in her life, she who'd had to learn to adjust to the knowledge that she couldn't have him, she who then had wanted him more than ever—she was what *he* now needed, in order to figure out where he'd gone wrong and, maybe, how to make it right.

So she would go see him at the inn. Or she would not go see him at the inn. She hadn't decided. Or, really, she *had* decided, a hundred times, and changed her mind just as often. If Casey went there to see Will, she would be getting involved more deeply, continuing what had begun when he leaned forward and kissed her cheek this afternoon. But if she didn't go, she would always wonder: What if?

What if? What if it had been Will Combray and not Michael Becket whom she married? This was the question that Casey to this day still sometimes found herself wondering about, and this was the question to which she'd long ago resigned herself to never knowing the answer.

At the end of the summer, just under a year after Michael and Casey first became lovers, Michael went away for three weeks to work as an arts and crafts counselor at the Indian Lake summer camp in the Berkshire Mountains. It was a job he'd arranged right before their relationship began, never suspecting that by the time summer rolled around, he would have a girlfriend and that he wouldn't want to leave her yet. He would have to leave her soon enough, for in the fall he'd be going off to college at the Rhode Island School of Design, while Casey would live at home and take teacher's education classes at the State University at Albany. The separation in the fall would be difficult, they'd agreed, but they would write and talk on the phone and visit all the time. The separation this summer, though, in these last, bittersweet weeks, seemed particularly cruel, at least to Michael.

"I could call the camp and cancel," he said to Casey one afternoon, as they sat on the swing by the pond. "Tell them I've come down with some incurable disease."

"And what disease would that be?" she asked playfully.

"You," he said, smiling.

"No," she said, and the playfulness suddenly was gone. In its place now was practicality. "Don't call them and cancel. It would be irresponsible."

"Man, I have never been irresponsible in my entire life," said Michael. "You know? I've always been the steady one, the upright citizen, Mr. Do-gooder. Don't I ever get to goof off a little?"

"Sure," she said. "Absolutely. Just as soon as you get back."

And Casey hoped it would in fact be possible that when he returned home at the end of the summer from Indian Lake, they could briefly goof off together, just as they used to. Before she and Michael were involved, their entire relationship had been propelled by a certain ease and grace. They would call each other on the phone at night, even though they'd just seen each other in the yard or on the porch an hour or two earlier, and they would talk and talk about everything and nothing, sometimes for hours. Now it was all different. Now, when she wanted to write to Michael at Indian Lake, Casey had to struggle to fill a page of stationery with the news of her summer, and then to find a way to sign it. "Love, Michael," his letters always ended. "Thinking only of you," is what she usually decided on.

All of the naturalness that had been so much a part of their friendship was now replaced by a generic quality, something learned by watching other people in love. This is *work*, she thought, but she didn't realize the toll that the situation with Michael was taking on her until one day during her piano lesson, right in the middle of a Chopin étude, she suddenly heard Dorian Bradley say to her, "Where *are* you?"

Casey pointed uncomprehendingly to the place on the sheet music that she'd reached in her playing.

"No, no. Not there. *Here*," and Dorian pointed to Casey's head. "And *here*," and she pointed to her heart.

Casey knew exactly what she meant. She realized she had been playing the notes, not the music. Her fingering lacked feeling, passion. She admitted to Dorian that her mind was elsewhere that day and that she'd been going through the motions at the keyboard, and then she struggled to put into words why: what a burden it was to be someone's girlfriend.

"I'm just exhausted by it," Casey said. "The whole *effort* of it. Is that normal?"

Dorian, sitting next to her on the bench, regarded Casey for a moment, then gestured with her head across the living room, toward the coffee table, where Casey's mother had set a tray of snacks that she'd baked. "Time for a break," Dorian said.

After they'd settled on the couch and they'd each filled a plate with lemon squares, Dorian said, "Do you know what you are, Casey?"

"No," said Casey uncertainly.

"You're a romantic," said Dorian.

Isn't everyone? Casey wanted to ask. She wasn't sure she understood, but when she was around Dorian she preferred to wait and see what her piano teacher had to say.

"You're very much like me," Dorian went on. "Your biggest problem is that you don't want to give yourself completely over to love until it feels as though you have no choice."

"Exactly!" said Casey. As soon as Dorian had said it, Casey knew it was true: Loving Michael had been a choice. A *decision*. She had decided to love Michael after being confronted by his kiss. It was so simple, this insight, so obvious, that Casey had to wonder how she'd missed it. But she knew how: because she'd wanted to. And then Casey broke down and cried, right there on the living room couch in front of Dorian Bradley, and while her piano teacher tenderly placed an arm around her shoulders, Casey couldn't help wondering what, and how, she was ever going to tell Michael.

As it happened, she didn't have to. One afternoon later that same week, when Casey ambled downtown in the heat to buy some ice cream, she noticed that a boy was watching her. Actually, he was sort of a boy and sort of a man, but in her mind she dubbed him a boy, for the word "man" seemed too formed and cooled for what he was. Out of the corner of her eye she could see him leaning against the Savings and Loan Building. He was smoking a cigarette and just looking at her, as brazen as anything, not even trying to pretend he was doing something else. She knew, or at least had been told, that she was a good-looking girl, slender and coltish, her hair wild. But because she'd been thinking of herself as belonging to Michael Becket over the past few months, she'd forgotten that anyone else might be interested, that anyone else might look and look.

He was no one she'd ever seen before; she'd have certainly remembered if she had. Casey walked more briskly down the street, listening to the heels of her Swedish clogs clacking on the pavement, knowing that the sound they made was a nervous, female sound. Not a skittish female but its unfortunate opposite: clunky. It was, she thought, the sound of a woman who doesn't know how to run away.

She wished she could have been more nonchalant about the whole thing, barely acknowledging his presence and just gliding away from him like a swan. But it was he who was seemingly uncaring. She could hear his quieter, slower steps, following her at a distance, at a leisurely pace, as if he had all the time in the world. When she got to the corner, she turned and glanced at him. They stood about twenty feet apart from each other, in front of Kessler's Five and Dime, with its out-of-date front window jammed with steam irons and can openers.

"Hello there," he said.

"Do I know you?" said Casey, knowing full well she didn't.

"My name is Will Combray," he offered, and then he smiled. "Now you know me."

"But you don't know *me*," said Casey. "So it's not reciprocal."

"Then tell me something about yourself," Will went on. "And then I'll know you."

"Like what?"

"Anything you want. Your name, for instance."

"Vanilla," she said.

"Your name is Vanilla?" the boy said doubtfully.

"No, I decided to tell you my favorite flavor instead," said Casey.

"Okay, good," Will said. He took a drag on his cigarette, then said, "Gustave Flaubert."

Despite herself, Casey found that she was smiling as well. "Your favorite writer," she said.

So: He was charming, this aggressive stranger who loitered on street corners, and he seemed intelligent and engaging. As casually as could be, he stubbed out his cigarette and asked her if he could walk her home.

"How do you know I live here?" she asked him.

"Of course you live here," he said. "Where else would you live?"

"I should be offended by that," she said. "I could live anywhere I choose, you know."

"Yeah, but you don't," said Will. "That's the thing, isn't it? You live here in this small town, this is where you live, and you fit right in. I bet you have a boyfriend, too. Probably known him your entire life or something, am I right? But only recently the two of you decided to change things a little, right? To start making out and being all passionate with each other."

"Get lost," Casey said, starting to turn away.

"How do you know I'm not lost already?" he said. "After all, I'm not from around here."

Casey felt her face grow hot. "You're an extremely rude person, you know," she said, turning her back to him.

"That may be," he conceded. "But I'm intuitive, too. I get these hunches, and I go with them. And I took one look at you and figured out the whole story."

Was she that predictable? Could a stranger take one look at her, see the jeans and the flowing blond hair and the Indian-print blouse, and know everything? Apparently, this stranger could.

"Come on, that kind of intuition has got to be worth *something*," he went on. "Besides, I followed you. You. Out of all the people in this town."

"So I should feel flattered?"

"Well, it's better than feeling insulted," he said, offering her a touchingly lopsided smile.

The Fountain

~

She studied him hard for the first time now, trying to look beyond the obvious details—the hair, the musculature beneath the T-shirt. And in fact there *was* more to him, for under his arm was a battered notebook.

He saw her glancing at it and said, "My journal."

"Oh, so you're going to be the next Gustave Flaubert," she said, laughing a little.

He shrugged and looked away, almost as if he were embarrassed.

"I'm sorry," she said. "I shouldn't have laughed."

He shrugged again, still looking off across the town square into the distance. "It's just notes and impressions and, you know, ideas for stories and poems and stuff. Probably not any good." He turned back and looked at Casey. "But you never know until you try, right?"

"Are you a student?" she asked him. "Do you study literature or something?"

Will shook his head. "I used to be a student, once, all the way up by the Canadian border. Until they asked me to leave, told me I wasn't doing much to advance the cause of education." He smiled again. "So I said okay. Then I got on my bike and left."

"Your bicycle?"

Will cocked his head. "Are you seriously that innocent, or is it all a mind game of some kind? Because I'm having a little trouble figuring you out."

"Think what you like," she said, wondering where the words came from, the teasing tone that she had adopted with him, as though it were second nature. She'd never spoken this way to anyone—and certainly never to Michael—yet she seemed to know exactly how to do it, to be a bit of a flirt, a tease, an arch and withholding girl who, if you were somehow able to capture her, would make you feel you were incredibly lucky to have done so. It was almost as though this stranger had known she would behave this way. Maybe, Casey thought, he brought this out in women; perhaps the most serious, studious, uninterested girl in the world would find herself adopting an ironic tone when she spoke to Will Combray and letting him think she was interested.

Or maybe this was who Casey really was.

"Okay, Vanilla," said Will. "I'll think what I like." He waited a second. "Are you going to tell me your real name?" he asked. "Or do I have to call you Vanilla forever?"

"Casey," she said after a beat.

"Nice to meet you, Casey," he said, extending his hand, as if acknowledging that the little game they'd been playing was over. "Look, I'm not staying around here or anything. I'm just driving through on my bike. My motorcycle, I mean. Don't worry, I'm no Hell's Angel or anything, and it's just a piece of junkyard garbage, but I've grown attached to it, and I'm kind of wandering around the country before I have to figure out what it is I want to do with my life for real. I was just planning on sleeping in a field somewhere, because the weather's still pretty warm at night. But listen, while I'm here in town, can I take you out?"

"Take me out?" she said. "You're telling me you don't even have a place to stay. Do you have any money, even?"

"Enough," he said. "You tell me where we should go, and I'll take you there."

She thought for a moment. "Okay," she said. "You're on. The Granary."

Casey had named the one expensive restaurant in town, an impulsive gesture not only because it cost too much money but also because they would be seen together there and talked about for days. *Did you hear? I saw Michael Becket's girlfriend, Casey Stowe, having dinner at The Granary with a strange boy. And they looked very comfortable together, if you get what I'm saying. . . .* The idea of people gossiping about her was appalling, but was it any worse, really, than the things people already said about how Michael and Casey looked so adorable together and how everyone knew they'd get married one day, because it was really meant to be—or else why would fate have placed those families right next door to each other on Strawberry Street?

"I'll meet you at that restaurant tonight at eight," Will Combray was saying to her, his husky, slightly rasping voice eclipsing the chorus of imaginary voices in her mind. "And don't worry, I won't do anything to embarrass you. It's strictly dinner. A meal. Two grown people breaking bread across a table, okay?"

This helped to remind her that in fact they were practically adults now. Although Casey often still felt quite young, living in the room she'd grown up in, with all the stuffed animals lined up on the bed, by any biological or legal standard Casey Stowe was fully grown. She was an adult, and she could do as she pleased, and so she heard herself saying to this stranger named Will Combray who was just passing through town, "Sure."

That night, excusing herself from the house after picking at the meal her mother had cooked—chicken breasts in a cream sauce, rice pilaf, broccoli, and pecan pie—Casey started to walk out of the house. "Where to?" her father asked as he watched her pull a sweater across her shoulders.

"Oh, just out, Dad," she said.

Warren Stowe was sitting in the living room reading the newspaper. He put the paper down across his lap for a moment, lifted his reading glasses from his eyes, and observed his daughter. "Well, you look very nice," he said, and she knew that it wasn't really a compliment. He wanted to know what she was doing, and she didn't want to tell him. So Casey left the house while her mother did the dishes and her father read the paper. As she walked past the house next door, she saw that Tom and Janice Becket were sitting on their front porch, he smoking a pipe and reading a magazine and she knitting something for some distant cousin who'd had a baby, a fact that Casey knew about from one of Michael's letters.

"Hello, Casey," Janice Becket called out.

"Hello, Mrs. Becket," said Casey, and she sternly told herself, Don't stop to talk to them, because if you do, they'll mention some little thing about Michael that will make you feel too guilty to go out tonight with Will Combray. "Have a nice evening," she added, ensuring there wouldn't be an extended conversation. Michael's parents mildly watched her go but didn't say anything.

The Granary was crowded by the time Casey got there, though she was relieved not to recognize anyone in the room. Will Combray was waiting at a table in the back. He had dressed for the occasion, she saw: a white Mexican wedding shirt with stitching on the edges. He looked up when the hostess brought Casey to the table.

"Hello, Vanilla," he said. "You look good tonight."

"Where'd you get that shirt?" Casey asked, sliding into her seat across from him. "Did you ride your bike all the way to Mexico this afternoon?"

"Oh, yes," he said. "And back. I picked up a piñata for you while I was there. Blue works well on you, by the way. I bet everyone wondered where you were going tonight. What did you tell them?"

The Fountain

ॐ

"Actually," Casey admitted, "I didn't tell them anything. Though I have no reason to lie, do I?" she added.

"I don't know," Will said. "You know the answer to that better than I do."

She thought for a moment. The waitress brought a basket of warm bread, and Casey slowly broke off a piece. "I do have a boyfriend, as you guessed this afternoon," she said. "His name is Michael Becket."

"And?"

"And what?" she said, popping a piece of crust into her mouth and trying to act casual.

"Well, that's answer enough, I suppose," he said.

"I've known him forever, as you also guessed, if that's what you mean," said Casey. "And I have absolutely no idea what I'm doing here with you right now."

"Maybe," Will said, "you came because you wanted to discuss Flaubert's use of a shifting point of view in *Madame Bovary*."

"Yes, maybe that's it," she said, trying not to smile.

"God, you're beautiful," Will Combray suddenly said, and the bluntness, the change in subject, the intensity—it was suddenly too much. It all hit her like

77

a strange pain that bunched up and then opened in-side her. They hadn't even ordered their dinner yet, and she wasn't at all hungry, couldn't tolerate the idea of eating tonight, or even of having a plate of food set before her.

"Please," she said, "can we go?"

His look of concern surprised her, and pleased her, too. Then Will nodded, laying down a mess of bills on the table, and with hasty apologies to the waitress and then the hostess, who stood at the front of the restaurant behind a lectern with a little light on it, they left. The night air felt chillier now.

"I was just playing, back there in the restaurant," Will said, after they'd walked a couple of streets in silence.

"It's okay," she said. Casey slipped her arms into the sweater that was draped around her shoulders. "It wasn't you."

"It was just a little teasing," he said. "Though not all of it. Not the 'God, you're beautiful' part."

"Shh," she said, and she boldly took his hand. And then, resuming the silence, they walked and walked. She had his hand, but it was he who was leading her. They were going somewhere, that much

78

was clear, but she didn't know where. Instead, Casey surrendered herself to winding roads that she didn't know. Maybe it was just the darkness, but she couldn't escape the sensation that even though this was her hometown, and she had lived here all her life, somehow Will was taking her to a place she couldn't recall ever seeing. Once in a while a car passed them, its *swoosh* lifting the ends of her hair slightly. Finally, she found herself in a field some-where, and there was moonlight surrounding them, and Will Combray's motorcycle stood alone, resting on its kickstand beside an army blanket that had been spread out on the grass. There was a knapsack on the blanket, and it was open. She could see a few things that were spilling out from inside it: books, a pocket knife, a greengage plum, a collapsible drink-ing cup, the type used by campers in the woods.

He was a traveler, a man living in a field, at least for now, but she knew he wasn't a real vagrant, and that he possessed a good mind, and that he was the most interesting person she'd met—not that she'd met all that many people in her nearly eighteen years, certainly very few who weren't from Long-wood Falls.

ॐ

"So where's that piñata you bought me in Mexico?" she asked quietly.

He smiled that crooked smile, and she noticed that his eyes were gray and catlike. They half closed as he took her hand and pulled her against him. He kissed her then, but not with the studied tenderness she was used to with Michael. This was something else entirely, a kiss that seemed to wrap her up inside of it. Soon the kiss was changing, expanding, including her whole body within it. She was afraid of the kiss, afraid of what it said about her, the way it told her that she was a girl who required something more than studied tenderness, a fact that she might never have known, and might never have needed to know, if Will Combray hadn't passed through Longwood Falls that day, on his way to who knew where.

Over the next couple of weeks, Casey slipped away to be with him all the time. She rode on the back of his bike, holding her arms around his waist and feeling the tightness of the muscles that were banded there, liking the sensation of the wind flooding her hair and the awareness of every bump in the road. She still wrote to Michael at Indian Lake, but her heart wasn't in the letters. She would have to tell him the truth eventually, the next time he came home, though it didn't seem right to do it in a letter, or over the telephone. In the meantime, Eleanor and Warren Stowe were disturbed by their daughter's strangely secretive behavior. They knew better than to confront Casey directly with their questions and concerns, and they certainly knew better than to breathe a word of it to the Beckets.

"What's going on, babe?" Eleanor asked her daughter one night after dinner, when Casey was in her bedroom getting ready to go out for the third evening that week. "We barely see you anymore. I know this is summer, and you're old enough to do what you like, sweetie, but Mrs. Jeffers over at the Cottonwood Dairy Market asked me the other day who was that boy she saw you with."

Eleanor Stowe was a pretty woman, had always been pretty, though in an understated way. She was shy, too, and she felt more comfortable in her own home with her family and the Becket family than anywhere else. When there was strangeness in the house—like now, with Casey acting odd and distant—then Eleanor felt deeply unsettled. Casey studied her mother for a moment, then turned away.

"I know she wasn't talking about Michael," Eleanor continued.

Casey turned back to her mother again, and suddenly there were tears shining in her eyes. "Oh, Mom," she said, "I don't know what's happening to me. But something is."

"What's the matter?" Eleanor asked with alarm. "Are you in some sort of trouble? Whatever it is, you can tell me, and I'll help you."

"Well, I guess I am in trouble," Casey said, choking on the words a little, "but it's not the way you think. I mean, I'm not pregnant or anything like that, in case you were worried. It's just that I've met a boy—a man, I guess. I don't know what he is, really, or even who he is. He's extremely mysterious, and I never know exactly where he's going or where he's spent the night or what kinds of things he's thinking about. He rides a motorcycle, and he writes in a journal all the time because he's always noticing all the little things that nobody else does, and he talks in the strangest way, and he and I can't seem to leave each other alone. It's as though we have to be together, Mom, as though everything will feel all wrong if we're not. I think about him all the time. Oh, I know this is awful, and that if Michael heard this conversation he'd be furious with me, but what can I do?"

Eleanor just stared at Casey for a moment, her face gone pale. Shakily, she sat down on the edge of her daughter's bed, where a few stuffed animals and rag dolls lay in a heap. She picked up one of the rag dolls, as though she needed to cling to the vestiges of Casey's childhood. Casey, too, couldn't help thinking about when she and Michael were little and used to play together in this room, sitting on the floor, creating entire miniature worlds that included only them.

"Well, honey," Eleanor said, "I don't really know what to say. Your father and I have been so pleased watching you and Michael grow up so beautifully together and eventually fall in love. It seemed so natural all along, not something that we'd pushed on you but something that you'd both found on your own. I suppose I have to accept that what you and Michael have together isn't right for you." She drew a breath. "But when you tell me about how this other . . . person makes you feel, it's almost as though you've been possessed."

"Yes! Exactly," said Casey. "That's just the way I feel. Like I've been possessed by Will, like I'm under a weird spell, like I'm not in charge of any of these feelings."

"And I'm not sure I know this girl you're talking about," said her mother, "a girl who seems willing to throw away such a wonderful relationship for one that seems so odd and uncertain. I mean, really, Casey, who is this boy, this *Will?* Do you know anything about him other than the fact that he obviously appeals to you . . . physically? There *is* more to life than having a good-looking face and being able to kiss well."

Casey studied her mother in the yellow lamplight of her bedroom, and all at once she thought she looked older. Her mother couldn't help her; no one could. What she was going through was something solitary, unreachable even by a concerned mother. Casey would just have to see this thing through and follow it in a state of trust and rapture, the way she had done when Will led her that first night down to a moonlit field. She was on her own. Nobody else could guide her now, not even her mother—especially not her mother, whom she loved so much and who

The Fountain

⌇

wanted only for her to be happy—just so long as that
happiness included the boy next door.

As each day passed, Casey became more and more
convinced there was no decent or acceptable way to
tell Michael what had happened to her. She was totally absorbed by Will, who was always available to
her and who seemed to exist like a strange, wandering apparition, sleeping in fields or motels or, most
recently, a room in a boardinghouse on the edge of
town, and telling her only fragmented details about
himself. She knew that he had grown up on the Canadian border, the son of a French-Canadian father who
worked at a lumber mill, and that his mother was a
housewife. She knew that Will spoke both French and
English and that he wanted to be a writer.

Sometimes he read some of his journal entries to
her in the room he'd rented in the boardinghouse. It
was a tiny, shabby room with a ripped window
shade and a gooseneck lamp of low wattage. The
bed was narrow, the mattress as thin and bumpy as
the road from the back of Will's motorcycle.

"'Today,'" he read aloud from the journal, "'I
woke up early and went down to the store and

bought my usual doughnut and milk. As I came back to my room with it, the powder from the doughnut left a trail on the floor, and old Mrs. L. scolded me. But I looked down at the dusting of sugar on the floor and thought how it was like a path leading up to my room, as though I wanted someone to follow it and find me. Because unless we leave trails behind, how will anyone know we were ever there? I sometimes think we need to be like slugs in the garden, leaving a wet, slippery trail behind us that says: I exist. I'm real. Follow me.'"

There on that bed, when he was done reading, Casey and Will made love for the first time, and as she slowly wrapped herself around him and got used to the feel of him against her, she cried because she'd betrayed Michael, and also, she had to admit, because she felt a depth of pleasure that she hadn't known was possible.

She hated to compare the two men, but it was inevitable; lovemaking with Will was so different than it had been with Michael. Michael was gentler and sweeter, seeking reassurances that he hadn't hurt her, that he wasn't rushing her. And she would answer, *No, no, of course not.*

The Fountain

And then there was Will. It was as if Will didn't need to ask. He knew. Will knew what he wanted, and he knew what Casey wanted, which was to be wanted by Will.

Was it an act, this slightly rough and indifferent attitude of Will's? If it was, it was an act that Will somehow knew Casey would like. For some reason she wanted him to behave as though he didn't care about her at first, when in fact she knew he did. The thrill for her was in sensing this indifference slowly transform itself into a kind of ardor, a need on his part that matched, by the end, the need on hers.

As for Michael, she still managed to fill pages of stationery with what books she was reading and the pieces of music she was learning during her piano lessons. And he, in turn, told her about the kayak trip he had taken his group of campers on, and about an emergency appendectomy one of the boys in the cabin had needed, but not about anything much beyond that. In their own way, his letters were as vague as hers. Was it possible? Maybe, she told herself, Michael had a girlfriend up there in the Berkshire Mountains, a female counselor who was pretty and athletic and with whom he shared late-night campfires. That would make it so much easier. But somehow Casey knew this wasn't likely. Michael was faithful—more faithful than she was, apparently.

"Dear Michael," she wrote to him one night, "this is so hard for me to tell you, but I really think it's time I did. . . ." And then she wrote it again two nights later, and then the night after that. And each time Casey would crumple up the letter and throw it out. She couldn't do this to Michael, so far away in his cabin, surrounded only by little boys and mosquitoes. It could wait, she decided, until she was able to tell him in person when he came home at the end of the summer.

As it would turn out, though, he would find out about it sooner. One night, after she'd walked with Will on the western edge of town, then kissed him in the darkness of the movie theater, where neither of them even noticed the thriller they were supposed to be watching, Will accompanied her all the way back to Strawberry Street. This was unusual; Will almost never went there, where he could be seen by Michael's parents or any of the neighbors. The hour was late, almost midnight; Casey knew that her own parents would be long asleep, and she guessed correctly that the Beckets would no longer be sitting out on their porch. The two houses, side by side, were dark. She and Will lingered for a while in front of her house, whispering and kissing, and then she took his hand. Now it was her turn to lead him, and where she led him was around the back of the house to the fountain. There, where the water played against the stone, Will Combray began to kiss her freely and easily, his hand slipping beneath her gauzy Indian cotton blouse with the tiny mirrors stitched into the fabric, his whole body leaning against hers, as he had done many times before.

What Casey didn't see was that Michael Becket had unexpectedly arrived home that night, and that right now he was sitting in the darkness of his family's back porch, watching everything, as silent and frozen as one of the stone angels in the fountain.

Chapter
Four

❧

∽ At the time, Michael felt he had been destroyed. It was only much later that he saw he hadn't
been, not really. He was whole, he was in one piece,
he was himself. Still, watching Casey with this other
man at the fountain had made him think, at first, *I
am dying*. He told Casey this, first thing the next
morning, as he sat in the Stowes' kitchen, con-
fronting her.

"I'm so sorry" was all she could say, hiding her
face in her hands. "I feel terrible about it. Just terrible. Oh, God. I didn't know . . ."

"That I'd come home?" Michael said sharply.

Casey looked up. "Well, yes. Yes, that. Exactly. I was going to tell you. Really, I was—"

"I was concerned about you," he said simply, his voice hoarse. "You sounded so distant in your letters. It was parents' weekend up at camp, and I asked if I could get away for a day, so I did. I didn't tell anyone I was coming. I thought I would surprise you. I guess I did," he added with a hollow laugh.

"I never meant for it to happen," Casey tried.

"For what to happen, Case?" said Michael with quiet rage. "The kiss itself, or me seeing it? Which is it, Casey?"

And she had to admit to herself that she really wasn't sure. For of course she had wanted the kiss to happen; she had wanted every one of Will's kisses last night to happen, just as she had wanted every moment of lovemaking in his room at the boarding-house to happen. She had become the kind of person for whom love, once experienced, becomes as necessary as water. It was what she'd always wanted, and it was what she'd never felt with Michael. Even now she couldn't help thinking that at the end of the day, when all this was over—this scene with Michael and whatever was to follow with his parents or hers—

she would be back in the arms of Will and that, yes, she couldn't wait for it to happen.

So she let Michael rage at her. Besides, what could she possibly say to satisfy Michael that wouldn't be a lie? *No, I don't love Will? No, I don't find him more exciting, more passionate, more . . . what?* The word returned to her, then, the word that Dorian Bradley had once used about Casey: "romantic."

"Tell me what I should have been doing all along," Michael was saying plaintively now. "What I could have done so this wouldn't have happened."

"There's nothing," Casey said. "Nothing you could have done, believe me."

"Then why?" said Michael. "For God's sake, Casey, why?"

"I don't know why," she said quietly. "Things happen, you know? And sometimes they're out of our hands."

"This was in your hands," Michael said with deadly calm.

"Yes and no," she said. "Okay, Michael, you're right. I let it happen. I did. I guess I wanted it to. But only because you and I were better together when we were friends, don't you think so?"

"No," he said. "I don't. I really don't. We would have become a very good couple, and it would have all worked out. It just needed time. We were going to write to each other this year, and visit each other, and spend vacations together—"

"But neither of us had ever been involved with anyone before," said Casey. "It was our first experience with this kind of thing. We didn't know what else was out there."

"*Who* else, you mean," said Michael.

Casey didn't answer, and after a moment, Michael's shoulders sagged.

"You make it sound as if it was a total failure, what we had," said Michael. "And it wasn't. We loved each other. We've loved each other forever. Look, Casey, let me ask you something." He leaned forward, resting his elbows on his knees, as if he could win her back by the force of reason. "Can you really tell him whatever's on your mind? Can you really know that he knows you almost as well as you know yourself?"

"No," she said. "I can't." She paused. "But the thing is, I actually don't want to."

Michael just sat there for a moment, unmoving,

just looking at her. Then he straightened in his chair. "Well, I don't know what I'm supposed to say to you now," he said finally. "I really don't. I thought you, me—you know. And now it's, it's—" He shook his head.

All Casey could say to him was, again, "I'm sorry."

He kept shaking his head slowly, and then he stood up like an old man. She heard one of his joints pop lightly, like the first kernel of corn in hot oil. "I have to go," he said. "They're expecting me back at camp. It's skit night tonight. Lucky me."

"But you've only just come home," said Casey, suddenly scared to see him go, to let him leave knowing how angry he was with her, how badly she'd hurt him, and knowing she could no longer count on him. She'd always counted on him—he was her source of comfort night or day—and now she'd traded in all of that for something unknown. If only he'd never kissed her, setting everything in motion. Why couldn't she have him for her best friend and also have Will for her lover? It was what she'd imagined might still be possible after the end of the summer, at least before Michael had shown up on her doorstep this morning to inform her of what he'd witnessed the night before. But now there was no chance of any remotely civil solution emerging from this situation, and the next thing she knew, Michael was brusquely walking out the kitchen door and heading across the yard and past the fountain.

Later in the day, Casey crossed the yard over to the Beckets' to apologize again, but Michael was already gone. Tom Becket stood in the doorway behind the screen when she showed up, looking out at her.

"He's off, Casey," he said mildly, this man who might someday have been her father-in-law.

"Please, Mr. Becket," Casey tried, "I don't know what Michael told you, but—"

Tom Becket held up a hand. "Casey," he said, "stop. What goes on between you and Michael is your business. I know that your mother and my wife tend to get very wrapped up in these matters, as though they're part of a living soap opera, but I try hard to stay out of it. No matter what happens, I'll still be your neighbor. And your friend."

"Thank you," she said in a tiny voice, and then she turned around and hurried home. Tom Becket was such a decent man that Casey had to do everything in her power not to cry in front of him. And she had to wonder whether, despite Tom's reassuring words, she hadn't lost not just Michael but the whole Becket family.

Even in her own house, her parents seemed awkward and embarrassed in front of her. She would enter a room where her mother and father were sitting and find it oddly silent, as though she'd walked into a conversation about her. She couldn't avoid the feeling that she'd let them down. It had never occurred to her before how important her role was, how much other people's happiness rested with her. Everyone was angry with her now, though only one of them—Michael—would admit it. But even he had made it clear that he wanted her to be a certain way, wanted her to feel things she didn't feel—that he would have preferred her to be fake.

There was only one person who didn't: Will. He wanted her just to be herself. He didn't need her to be a certain way in order to please him. So she called him now, asking the crabby old woman who ran the boardinghouse if she could speak to him. When he got on the phone, Casey told him she needed to see him, and he said she could come right over. And suddenly she was lying against him, crying quietly into the soft cotton of his T-shirt, telling him how terrible she felt about hurting Michael, but how smothered she felt by everyone's expectations. "I feel like I'm suffocating," she said.

"Come here, you," he said, pulling her even closer and making her realize that he was the only one whose touch wasn't overwhelming. His need for her made her feel calm. He spoke to her softly, reassuringly, and after a while his words and the touch of his hands became arousing to her. She found herself kissing him over and over, forgetting all about Michael Becket and what had happened last night by the fountain, and feeling as if here, within the walls of a nondescript room in an anonymous boardinghouse, was home, because here was Will.

Getting married was Will's idea, though Casey had been quietly fantasizing about it, too. They had been lying in his bed for the better part of a Saturday afternoon that autumn. Casey had a college textbook open in front of her, to a chapter devoted to the theory of teaching phonics to first-graders, but she'd barely looked at it, even though a paper based on the material was due in three days. She'd begun college in a distracted fashion—she who'd always been such an animated and eager student in high school. The truth was, none of her college courses were half as interesting as Will. More often than not, reading gave way to making love. That had been what had happened today, and now he propped himself up on an elbow and said, "Hey, Vanilla?"

"Mmm?" she replied.

"Will you marry me?"

Casey looked at him sharply. "Don't joke about something like that, Will."

"I'm not joking," he said.

"So, what—you're really proposing to me?" she said, her voice rising up with a kind of alarm.

"I suppose that's exactly what I'm doing," said Will. "Proposing. I've never done that before."

"I don't take it lightly," Casey said.

"Me neither," he said. "I don't take it lightly at all. I'm serious about this. I know, I know. We're young. But what can I say? I want to. I have no idea what I'll do for money to support my writing habit, but I can get a job, and we can find ourselves a place not too far away—maybe in the next town—so you don't have to uproot yourself. We can rent one of those little cottages in Westindale, near the river. You can drive down to Albany for school, and I'll work at some laborer's job all day and write at night. And you'll become a teacher, and with a little luck, I'll become a famous novelist or poet." He took her hand in his and kissed the individual fingers. "I love you," he said quietly. "You really know yourself, don't you? You know that you want to be a teacher—and I'm sure you'll be great at it—and you've got this terrific family that believes in you. Me, my father couldn't care less how I end up, since it's clear to him I'm not going to join him up there in logging country, thank God. I'm on my own, and there are times when it's too much for me. But then I think about being with you, settling down together, starting a little life that will feel calm and consistent and made up of days like today—just the two of us lying in bed like this—and I know it feels right. So I'll ask you again: Will you marry me?"

She paused for a moment, so she wouldn't seem too compliant, and then she quietly said, "Yes," and he kissed her hard on the mouth. She felt the rough bristle of his unshaven chin, slightly pleasurable and slightly painful, and there it was, she thought: love. With Michael, she hadn't felt any pain. Until she'd ended things with him, there had been no hint of it; all was sun-filled and improbably hopeful, exactly what you'd want from a lifelong friend, but not—at least from Casey's perspective—what you'd want from your lover.

"You're my life," said Will.

Later, lying in her own, much softer, bed, surrounded by ancient stuffed animals and the posters on the walls and the muffled sounds of her parents' conversation from somewhere in the house, this was what she kept returning to: how, when you agreed to marry someone, you became part of his life, and he yours. For Will, that life so far had been rootless and ungrounded by a real sense of family; now *she* would be his family. For Casey, that life so far had been nothing *but* family, claustrophobically so; now she would be free to make her own family. And in that new family, that family of two, Casey believed, she would *breathe*.

And it was in fact the open air that she always

thought of when she imagined their life together: breezing through the countryside on the back of his old bike, or camping out in a field under the open sky, the two of them reading aloud to each other. And at night, in their little cottage in Westindale, they would lie in front of the fireplace and tell each other things they'd never told anyone before. They would drink each other in, the way newlyweds did.

" 'Drink each other in'?" her mother said with distaste when Casey had sat her parents down in the living room to tell them of her plans. "What on earth has happened to you, Casey? Just listen to you. It's as though this Will Combray has changed your personality."

"Please, Mom and Dad. Don't you see?" Casey said. "I'm finally happy."

"We thought you were happy with Michael," her mother said.

"No, Mom, *you* were happy with Michael," Casey shot back. "You and Mrs. Becket were so excited about the whole thing that you forgot about me, and what I want. Besides," she went on, "it's not like I'm dropping out of college or something. And it's also not like I'm rushing into it, either. Will and I have agreed that we should wait until next summer to get married, so that we can do it right. In the backyard, with flowers everywhere."

"Well! Thank heaven for small favors," said her father.

Some part of Casey recognized how absurd she must be sounding, yet she couldn't stop herself. How could she possibly describe to her parents all the things she was feeling about Will? The fact was, she couldn't. Instead, Casey took a deep breath and simply said, "Please try to understand. Just try? For me?"

"Understand?" her mother said. "You're *eighteen*, sweetheart."

"But I'll be nineteen by the time we get married. And you and Dad got married at that age," said Casey.

"But," said her father, "there's a tremendous difference between the world today and how it was back then. When your mother and I got married . . . well, that's what people *did*. But now, honey, you don't *have* to. You can explore the world. Spread your wings a little. You can wait until the time is right. Of course," he quickly added, with a glance toward Eleanor, "the time was right for us when we got married."

"Well, next summer the time will be right for Will and me, too," said Casey.

At this, her father softly bit his lip and looked away, and her mother began to cry quietly. Her parents had met Will, if only briefly, and the impression he'd made on them hadn't been exactly what Casey had hoped. Will had sat in their living room, had answered their questions with obvious discomfort, had eaten their food and said please and thank you. He'd behaved in a perfectly respectable if unremarkable manner, and Casey knew that his charms were lost on her parents. She could see it in their eyes, written in the subtle language of significant looks that couples cultivate over the decades: *He's not Michael.*

He's not even Will, she wanted to scream back at them. This wasn't Will, this polite and subservient guest sitting on the couch with a napkin on his knee. What *was* Will was wild and free and unpredictable and—

And what was the point, already, of depositing the charms of Will on these deaf ears?

"Would you prefer we got married at City Hall? Now?" Casey said in a slightly formal tone. "We could, you know."

"Oh, God," her father muttered.

"Case," her mother said. "Casey. Look. If you really feel this way about Will, and I think your father agrees with me on this"—here Eleanor exchanged a glance with Warren, as if to ascertain that this thin ice onto which she was now treading wasn't going to swallow her whole, and alone—"then I'm sure we could find it in ourselves to arrange a wedding in the backyard here. And I'm sure it would be perfectly lovely," she added, shooting another look at her husband, "don't you think, Warren?"

"Lovely," said Warren Stowe.

And so Casey was to be married in the summer. Her impending wedding was all the talk in town, at least among her mother's set of friends and among girls Casey knew who still lived at home. Suddenly, the odd, old-fashioned courtship of Casey Stowe and Michael Becket was replaced by the far more fascinating prospect of Casey Stowe's marrying a terrific-looking mystery guy who hailed from far away and wanted to be a writer.

Not surprisingly, under the circumstances, Michael kept his distance, both literally and figuratively. After he'd returned from Indian Lake for good, he'd spent a week at home packing for college, and then he was gone: gone from the street, from the town, from Casey's life. They'd said a quick good-bye the day his parents drove him up to Providence for freshman orientation, but neither of them could bear to look the other in the eyes. Casey felt ashamed; Michael felt betrayed. It was a bad combination.

And now his parents must have certainly told him about her engagement to Will Combray. They would have broken it to him gently, perhaps over the phone or during one of their visits to Providence. How would Michael have reacted? Casey wondered. With shock, certainly, and with deep sadness. And then, knowing Michael, he would have thrown himself even further into his work. Casey wished that she'd been able to tell him herself, but she hadn't been in touch with him since college had begun, knowing that he needed time away from her, time to start feeling better after having been hurt so deeply by her. The news about the wedding would hurt all over again, she understood, and all she could hope was that up there in his college town, Michael had met another girl. An art student, someone easygoing and kind, who was excited by everything about him. Someone who would love him the way he deserved to be loved.

As the months passed, Casey saw Michael occasionally when he came home from college for a visit. He would nod hello to her, and she would nod back, and once he even congratulated her on her upcoming wedding. There was a flatness to his voice when he said this, an absence of sarcasm or anger. It was as though all the feeling Michael had once had about Casey had been drained out of him. What they'd once had was over, done with, he seemed to say, and all that was left was the faintest trace memory of a happier time.

When the invitations went out for the Stowe-Combray wedding (there was no question that all the Beckets would be invited, given that the wedding would be held literally in their yard), Michael's response card came back with the acceptance box checked off. The Stowes and the Beckets no longer socialized as often as they used to; how could they, when there was such unhappiness between the children? The fountain, of course, still stood, a symbol of solidarity that had outlived its usefulness. Yet it *stood*, and as much as both sets of parents may have wished that they had never torn down the hedge between the two houses, the fountain remained a handy centerpiece around which Casey could arrange her wedding ceremony: inconvenient, perhaps, yet undeniable.

A week before the wedding, Casey received a letter in the mail, and she immediately recognized the handwriting as Michael's. He had gone back to Indian Lake again this summer, but she'd seen him around town lately and knew he was at home for the period of time between the end of camp and the start of his sophomore year. Even though he was physically so close by, Michael apparently preferred to deliver his message in writing. Trembling, barely able to jimmy the flimsy flap, Casey fumbled with the envelope for several agonizing seconds until, finally, she'd succeeded in opening it.

The Fountain

⁂

It began:

Dear Casey,

I know I said I would be coming to your wedding. Unfortunately, I won't be able to attend. I could make up all sorts of excuses, but the truth is, I think it would simply be too painful for me. This is the kind of thing I suppose I could feel better about if I talked it over with a really close friend. But the problem is, you're the friend I would have chosen, the one I would have poured out my heart to about how it feels knowing you're getting married to Will. No offense against Will. I don't know him, so I can't say anything about him. This isn't about him, in fact, because I wish the two of you all the happiness in the world.

I wish I could describe the grief I've felt, and continue to feel, over losing your friendship. I remember once—it feels now like a long time ago—but I remember saying to you something about what a cliché it was to feel that I was losing my mind over you. Well, Case, I've got another cliché for you now—the cliché to end all clichés: I hope that, despite everything, we can still be friends.

Good luck on Saturday. You'll knock 'em dead with your beauty.

Love,
Michael

The ceremony was set for a Saturday afternoon at twelve, and for the hour preceding the wedding, cars began crawling along Strawberry Street, looking for places to park. Soon the street was entirely lined with cars, and some people even parked in the driveways and on the lawns of various neighbors, all of whom were invited. It was like a block party, friendly and festive, though tinged with the slightest air of murmured scandal, because the boy Casey Stowe was marrying wasn't Michael Becket.

With the modest sum of money that Casey's parents had given to the couple, they'd managed to take out a lease on a one-room cottage in Westindale. It was tiny, and the floor buckled in several places, and the furnishings that came with the place were depressing: a tweedy brown couch with a cigarette stain on one of the cushions, and a few ragtag tables and chairs. But still, it was theirs, ready for occupancy as soon as they came back from their "honeymoon," which would consist of a weeklong jaunt around the Northeast on Will's motorcycle, sleeping in camp-grounds under the stars in newly wedded bliss.

Will's parents came down from Canada for the occasion, his father a large, weary-looking man of massive strength and few words, his mother meek and small as a sparrow. Though neither the Beckets nor the Stowes were wealthy people, the Combrays, a man and woman who lived in a logging camp, seemed out of their element even here among the modest, neatly tended homes of Strawberry Street. Casey's parents tried to engage them in small talk— how nice it was that Casey and Will had met (a white lie), how well Casey and Will seemed to get along— but the conversations went nowhere fast. Eventually, Will's father simply turned to his wife and began speaking to her in rapid French, which struck Eleanor Stowe as perplexingly rude. Who *were* these people? Nobody seemed to know, and there was nobody to ask, since the only names on the invitation list, aside from those of the groom's parents, had belonged to the bride's side.

Who was Will Combray? The question simmered throughout the crowd on the morning of the wedding. For her part, Casey had always found that the best way to deal with Will's past was not to ask him too many questions. She'd long ago figured out that he didn't like to feel that he was being grilled or put on the spot—"pinned down," was how he phrased it—and she certainly saw no reason to expect any changes in the weeks leading up to the wedding. Instead, Casey waited for him to offer information about himself, which he did, sometimes.

The night before they were to be married, however, was one occasion when Casey did expect Will to give of himself, if only in the most superficial and public way. There was to be a dinner at her family's house; in recent weeks there had been several such occasions, slightly awkward affairs at which her mother became overly chirpy and frenetic, going on and on about the meal she had prepared, while her father turned taciturn.

But the one taking place the night before the wedding Will skipped. He said he needed to be alone, that he wanted to think about everything that was about to happen, and that he wanted to be well rested for the next day. Casey didn't even try to stop him. It would have been futile; that much she knew. And so, instead, she sat in her parents' kitchen, surrounded by family—father and mother, aunts and uncles and cousins who had traveled some distance to be in Longwood Falls for her wedding—yet miserably alone.

This was the final night she'd be living in this house on Strawberry Street, eating her mother's pecan chicken breasts and glazed baby carrots, and she looked around herself at the blur of faces she'd known since she was a baby and tried to imagine *not* living here. She'd be near enough to home, that was true, but for all intents and purposes, everything would be different. And then, through the kitchen window, a sudden movement caught her eye: Michael, walking with his father out to the car, both men dressed in their plumbers' boots and carrying toolboxes.

Tell me a story, Casey wished she would be able to say when Michael got back home later. *Tell me what you saw out there tonight in the big, surprising world.* And then she thought of Michael's letter to her a week earlier, and she wondered if what he said he now wanted, and what she'd so often wished for, was possible to achieve, and whether it would be enough for either of them: that they could remain friends.

That night, Casey barely slept. At seven in the morning, she rose from her bed and began the day. Bridesmaids fussed around her—Janine Phelps from high school and Laura Carozza from college, and cousin Sue from Pennsylvania, whom she loved but didn't see often. Casey's hair was arranged into intricate braids and knots, threaded through with seed pearls. The elaborate dress, purchased at Albany Traditional Bridal and far more expensive than Eleanor and Warren had imagined a dress would be, was held out by two bridesmaids so Casey could step carefully into it. Once it was on, she tried to stand absolutely still while cousin Sue buttoned the tiny buttons, but Casey found herself shaking all over, as if she were coming down with the flu. Even her mother, who had been upset at the prospect of this marriage from day one, finally surrendered to the emotion of the moment.

"You—" Eleanor said, shaking her head. Then she

tried again. "You are such a pretty bride. Will's going to take one look at you and thank his lucky stars he ever met you."

"He already does, Mom," she said.

"This is different," said Eleanor. "When your father and I got married, I didn't let him see me until the very last minute. He'd been in a kind of fog for the weeks leading up to the wedding—you know the way your father gets—and so I don't think he'd given much thought to what I would look like. I had described the dress endlessly to him, of course, but I'm not sure he ever really listened." Eleanor smiled to herself at the memory. "But there I stood in my wedding gown in front of the minister and all those dressed-up people, and your father looked at me, and his eyes seemed to bug right out of his head. It was as though he didn't even recognize me, or as though he'd never really seen me before that moment. He stood beside me and whispered, 'Eleanor, I can't believe what I'm seeing,' and it made me feel so . . . loved. As though all the thought I'd given to the day, all the preparation and the work and the million fittings for the dress—they had been worth it. Because I knew he cherished me, sweetheart. Just the way Will is going to cherish you."

"Oh, Mom," said Casey, inching forward in the rustling silk, folding herself into Eleanor's embrace, delicate so as not to crease the dress, yet somehow fervent in a way that Casey had never before experienced with her mother, "Thank you."

By five minutes before twelve, all the guests had assembled on the white chairs in the backyard. The fountain, which Tom Becket had cleaned out for the occasion, burbled fully and majestically. The minister, a bald and earnest man, stood beneath the angels, smiling noncommittally. A chamber trio, made up of musicians from the Albany Symphony Orchestra and hired for the afternoon as a wedding gift olive branch from Janice and Tom Becket, began to play. The day was clear and shot through with sunlight, and everyone said that the occasion was perfect.

Except for the fact that the groom had not arrived.

It took a while for anyone to notice, but eventually there was a buzz of conversation among the assembled members of the wedding party and then, inevitably, among the guests. But the rumor that at first seemed preposterous was true: Will Combray had not yet shown up. Even his parents hadn't seen him.

Quietly and without making a fuss about it, Warren Stowe went back inside the house and telephoned his future son-in-law's boardinghouse. Old Mrs. Lynchley answered on the fifteenth ring.

"Hello?" she said suspiciously, as though the phone were ringing in the middle of the night and the caller had some nerve. "Who is this?"

"I'm looking for Will Combray," said Casey's father. "He's expected at his wedding ceremony, and he hasn't shown up."

"Will Combray?" said the old woman, and she laughed harshly. "I'd like to see him, too, I would. He took off last night on that noisy, smelly motorcycle, cleared out without paying this week's rent. The room is bare. I don't know where he's gone."

Casey, who had followed her father into the house, looked at the expression on his face as he talked on the phone and knew that something had happened to Will. Something bad. "Oh, Dad," she said in a whisper, "is he dead?" She pictured a motorcycle accident, with Will sprawled on the side of the road somewhere, his body twisted and broken.

But her father was shaking his head. He hung up the phone and in a quiet voice said, "He's not dead, Casey. He's just gone."

"Gone?" She froze there in her white gown. Outside, the guests were restless and concerned, talking among themselves in increasingly loud voices. A few people stood up and peered across the lawn toward the windows of the house, trying to catch a bit of the drama that was going on inside.

"Yes," said Warren Stowe. "He's disappeared, honey. Checked out of his room last night, the woman said. I have no idea of where he's gone, but I want you to know that whatever happens, your mother and I are here for you, sweetheart."

Will had really jilted her. The truth was right there before her, plain as the faces staring back at her through the kitchen window. Who knew when Will had decided not to show up—weeks ago, or as recently as last night, when the prospect of what it might mean to be a married man hit him full force and he couldn't tolerate it?

And just as he could not tolerate marrying her, so could she not tolerate the idea that he would not be hers, that he had left her so grotesquely like this. She thought of all the people out there, sitting on their chairs, dressed in those nice clothes, bringing all those presents, and she thought of the endless preparations her parents had made. She pictured the trays of smoked-salmon finger sandwiches and the rows of buckets that held bottles of champagne buried up to their necks in ice. She pictured herself, a ludicrous figure in beautiful white silk and seed pearls, and then, before she could think about it for one second longer, Casey Stowe collapsed into the waiting arms of her father.

Chapter
Five

❧

After all the guests were gone and the tent was pulled down, long after the weeks passed and the gossip began to die away, Casey Stowe continued to stay inside her parents' house. She didn't want to see anyone, and she didn't want anyone to see her. The mix of humiliation and sadness was overwhelming; even her own parents adopted expressions of such intense sympathy whenever she sat with them at meals in the kitchen that she could hardly meet their eyes.

"Oh, darling," said her mother one night when the three of them sat at another stilted family dinner,

"I know you're still in shock, and I know you're still grieving, but one day you're simply going to have to let go of him."

Casey nodded in agreement, but couldn't really speak. She'd had no choice but to fall in love with him, and now, she supposed, she had no choice but to let him go. Will had disappeared and had never been heard from again. His own parents had no idea of where he'd gone, and they didn't seem particularly concerned. "He's always been like this; he comes and goes," Mr. Combray had said over the telephone when Casey's father called a few weeks after the canceled wedding, to see if Will had eventually turned up. "That's who Will is."

Yes, Casey supposed, that's exactly who Will is. That was the Will she'd fallen in love with. It was part of the attraction, part of the thrill, his mysterious and uncertain nature. But she'd thought that she and Will were united in it. She hadn't imagined—or hadn't allowed herself to imagine—that this same unpredictability could ever turn against her. And then she had to wonder just how well she'd known exactly who Will was, because the Will she thought she knew wouldn't have been capable of doing to anyone what he had done to her. *That* Will, she thought, was the man her parents had tried to warn her against, to shield her from, even after she'd insisted to them that that Will was someone she didn't know.

The lease on the cottage in Westindale had been broken, and someone else had rented the place. The life that Casey and Will had been about to invent together was now fading rapidly. She pictured them in the cottage, lying together on the terrible, springless brown couch or sitting in front of the fireplace drinking cups of fragrant Chinese tea. And then, after a while, the images receded, lost their shimmering Technicolor quality, then slowly disappeared.

One morning in early September, Casey was sitting in her bedroom, thinking about how to get through another sluggish day, when she heard the sound of voices and slamming car doors outside. She lifted the edge of her shade and peered through the window. There, in the driveway next door, was Michael Becket standing with his parents, loading the back of his family's truck with a steamer trunk and rolled-up posters and his Smith-Corona type-writer. He was going back to the Rhode Island School of Design, she knew.

Seeing him standing there in an old gray track sweatshirt and jeans, his father's arm draped lightly around his shoulders in a moment of wistful camaraderie, she felt an indescribable sensation. How quickly everything turned. A little over a year earlier, it had been Michael who yearned day and night for someone he couldn't have, while Casey saw the future with a sense of newfound, limitless freedom. Now their situations were exactly reversed. Michael, a young man on the verge of a new life, seemed to represent everything she, sitting idly in her dim childhood bedroom, had lost: hope and success and promise. She remembered what it was like being Michael's best friend when they were small, and then his confidante when they were older, and then, finally, imperfectly, his lover. All of it seemed like a sad dream right now, the kind that's irretrievable the moment you wake up. And it was she who had chosen to wake up, she who had chosen Will Combray over the vastly more appropriate—and apparently worthwhile—Michael.

The Fountain

As she gazed out at Michael through the window, he suddenly looked up from what he was doing and saw her. It was almost as if he couldn't leave without one last look in her direction, and she couldn't think fast enough to draw back, into the recesses of her bedroom. For a startling instant, their eyes held. What did he think of her right now? Did he find her pathetic? Did he feel a sense of victory over her? If so, it didn't show. Michael looked at her with an expression that was unreadable. Some part of her would have liked to shove up the window and call out to him, "Michael, wait. Before you go back to school, I need to see you." And then she would have rushed out of her depressing room and into the Beckets' driveway, embracing him and telling him she'd made a terrible mistake. But it was too late for that, and besides, it wasn't what she wanted.

What she wanted, though, didn't want her.

Quickly, Casey pulled down the shade, unable to look at him any longer. A little while later, when she heard the Beckets' truck pull away, Casey brought herself to look out the window once more, but this time all she saw was an empty driveway and a darkened house.

Casey had been reminded on countless occasions by her mother that time heals all wounds—Eleanor Stowe had said it so often that she sounded like a broken record—and while Casey wished she could believe her mother's words, she found it difficult to move on. At night she dreamed of Will, seeing him with that crooked smile and his sheaf of sandy hair falling in his face.

In her dream she imagined kissing him and letting him make love to her, slowly learning what felt good and what felt better. When she woke up from these dreams, she was sometimes gasping and confused. Will didn't love her, or love her enough, anyway; that was the real lesson she had learned from him, and though it was incredible to her, even now, she had to accept it as the truth. She had done something wrong; she hadn't been good enough, interesting enough, exciting enough, *something* enough for him. And because of it, she was stuck in her life, unable to imagine being without him. She took a leave of absence from college in Albany, knowing that she would barely be able to concentrate on her schoolwork. When she'd first fallen in love with Will, her academic life had suffered, but still she'd been able to coast along. Now, she knew, coasting wasn't an option; her sadness was too consuming for that.

One day, Casey received a note in the mail. It was from Dorian Bradley, who had written to her favorite former piano student to say good-bye. She would be moving away, to some city or another, though she wasn't sure which one; after all these years of complaining, she'd finally had enough of small-town life. Me, too, Casey thought, folding the letter and filing it in a drawer. But to her surprise, the loss in her life of the teacher with whom she'd once spent so many memorable, formative afternoons didn't add to Casey's gloom. Instead, she found what Dorian was doing somehow inspirational, as if her teacher, once again, were setting the example. That same afternoon, Casey wandered downstairs, sat at the piano in the living room, and began playing. It was a rough sound that she produced, she knew; she was out of practice. But it was music, and it was enough. Drawn by the sound, her mother appeared briefly in the doorway, and Casey hesitated in her playing and nodded once to her, as if to say, *I'm back*.

Eventually, Casey began venturing out of the

house once in a while, strolling, head down, the several blocks to the center of town. She shopped for clothes or stopped for ice cream, and as she did so, she began thinking about her future. In time, she applied for readmission next semester at the university. One day when she was downtown, she looked up and noticed that all of Longwood Falls was strung with Christmas lights.

Michael, she knew, would be coming home from college for Christmas vacation, and Casey wondered if it was really possible that the two of them, as they'd both once hoped, could somehow become friends again. The prospect of his return, Casey found, gave her something to look forward to, and every so often she caught herself glancing over toward the Beckets' house, watching for Michael. Then, two days before Christmas, she saw him. He was walking up the path to his house, coming from the direction of town.

"How's college going this year?" she called to him from her front porch, trying to sound casual.

Michael turned around, surprised. "Hi, Case," he called back. "Fine, thanks." After a moment's hesitation, he crossed the lawn, then stood at the bottom of the steps. He looked older now, handsomer, as though his face had finally grown into his features. He was wearing a coat she'd never seen before, long and thick, like something belonging to a character in a Russian novel. "How about you, Casey? How have you been?"

"Fine," she answered.

"Going to school?" he asked.

"No," she said, "I took some time off."

"Oh," he said. "Well, anyway . . ." He nodded his head, looked away toward his house, looked back toward Casey. "Well," he said again.

"Well."

"I've got to go, I guess," he said.

"Me, too," she said, rubbing her arms against the cold. "I'm in the middle of making dinner."

"Your folks out?" he said, looking at the Stowes' empty driveway.

"Yeah, they're picking up the Christmas tree," she said. "I'm making a roast chicken for when they get back. You're welcome to join us, if you want. The chicken's gigantic; we could feed an army."

"Thanks, Case, but I can't. I've already got this thing—"

133

"No, no, that's fine, of course," she said.

"But thanks anyway. Some other time."

"Sure," she said.

"Good. Well, see you."

"See you," she said. After another moment's hesitation, Michael turned away, and Casey watched him trudge back across the snowy lawn and into his parents' house before she went back into hers.

It was a start, anyway. He'd be home for a couple of weeks; she would see him again. She had no idea of what his life was like, really, although she heard the occasional academic detail from her mother, whose relationship with Janice Becket was, if no longer a close friendship, then at least cordial enough to include such news, dispensed when the women happened to run into each other.

Casey stopped at the phonograph player in the living room on her way back to the kitchen and picked out an old LP, a Nat King Cole Christmas album that she used to listen to with her parents when she was young. The music would remind her of happier, more hopeful times, of sitting in this very room with her parents and Michael and his parents, everyone talking and eating and feeling warm and close.

The Fountain

Nat was singing "Have Yourself a Merry Little Christmas" when the doorbell rang. The first thing Casey, standing at the sink washing lettuce, thought was, It's Michael. He's changed his mind. He'll be joining us for dinner after all. She dried off her hands and hurried to the door. But when she pulled it open, all she saw were the lights, which filled the street as they described sweeping arcs. Then, right in front of her, she took in the presence of the two state troopers. One of them, a woman, had a walkie-talkie that emitted grizzled static. They were standing there side by side, as though it took two people to bear the bad news they were certain to deliver. The dish towel fell silently to the floor from Casey's hands.

"Yes?" she said, but she already knew: There had been an accident. It was winter, and the roads were slippery on the way to the Zagajewski X-mas Tree Farm. Year after year, her parents always made the trip, and always they complained about the ice and the skidding, but always they returned home safely, a huge tree tied to the roof-rack of their station wagon. But not this year, Casey knew, even before she grimly opened the door wider and let the troopers in.

꒜

Casey didn't remember much of what happened afterward. She recalled that she wept for a long time and that she felt a kind of primitive anguish that coursed through her endlessly. But she had no idea of who spoke to her that night, of who came to the house and tried to help, of who led her to the couch when she felt dizzy. She remembered faces of neighbors, whispers, ringing phones, the jingling of the keys on the troopers' wide black belts, the nauseating smell of burned chicken. At some point, she remembered, Tom and Janice Becket appeared before her. They hadn't been inside the Stowes' house in some time, and now Tom Becket was standing beside the couch where Casey lay and asking in a formal, courteous tone, "Casey? May we come in?"

Casey looked up and nodded. Everything had a dreamlike quality to it that night, and she couldn't be sure what she and the Beckets said to one another, if anything, but what she did remember was being led, at the end of the evening, next door to the Beckets' house for the night.

"You'll sleep here, honey," Janice Becket said to her as they walked down the path to the sidewalk. "You can stay as long as you need to."

The Fountain

And though some part of Casey knew that it was strange to be in Michael's house again—and though she knew that Michael was there right now, too—none of it seemed to matter anymore. Nothing did. Whatever differences the two families had had, however distant she and Michael felt from each other—none of it mattered now. The past had been obliterated, wiped clean the moment her father lost control of his car on the road and slammed into a tree. What had been a bad year had suddenly transformed into an unimaginably tragic one.

Casey slept heavily that night, after one of the neighbors, a doctor, offered her a Valium to help her relax. It was only when morning arrived, and she woke up in a strange guest room to see the bright light of the sun reflecting off the snow, that she remembered what had happened. Her wonderful mother and father were gone. She tried to absorb this fact and couldn't. The father who would toss her into the air until she'd shriek with happiness when she was a little girl—gone. The mother, in the background, who would nervously murmur, "Warren, that's high enough"—gone. The parents who had paid for piano lessons, and taught her to think for herself, and lived long enough to wonder what they'd done so wrong that their eighteen-year-old daughter would want to get married and run off with Will Combray—gone.

It couldn't be true, she felt. It couldn't *not* be true, she knew.

She'd felt the same way, of course, when Will Combray had left, but there was a big difference. Will was somewhere on the Earth; he had just chosen not to be with her. Even right this minute, he was waking up, or going to sleep, or holding another woman in his arms. But Warren and Eleanor Stowe, God rest their souls—gone for good.

Casey realized, at that moment, that if Will were here, he would have helped her through this. This was what husbands and wives did for each other. He would have cradled her and protected her and stayed up long into the night with her, just to talk. He would have held her while she cried; he would have made her soup. He would have told her he loved her, over and over. But the truth was, of course, that he didn't love her—and that truth somehow made the loss of her parents even more unbearable. If only Will *had* loved her, then she might be able to get through this, somehow. But she was alone—more alone now than she'd ever been in her life. Whatever she was going to have to find it within herself to do, in her struggle to cope with the loss of her parents, she was going to have to find it on her own.

The funeral was a blur. All the details were handled primarily by Tom and Janice Becket. Practically the entire town crowded into the small church, and various people spoke on behalf of the Stowes, including Tom and Janice. Through her haze, Casey forced herself to listen closely, carefully, hoping to find some bit of wisdom she would be able to take away from this service, something she could turn to that might help her make sense of the days and weeks to come, as life went on, swallowing up her parents and turning them into a memory.

Toward the end of the funeral, it was Michael who suddenly stood up and walked to the podium. He was wearing a dark suit and tie, and he appeared nervous. He took a deep breath, and then he began.

"When I was a little kid," Michael said, "I had these next-door neighbors who were so close to our family that for a long time I literally thought they *were* my family. I felt, in some way, that I'd been blessed by being given an extra set of parents. Two people, Eleanor and Warren Stowe, who were always so easygoing and kind to me. Mrs. Stowe was a terrific cook, as most of you know, and she would make these pots of stew in the wintertime, and we'd all go over to the Stowe house and sit around the kitchen table eating and talking. Both my parents and the Stowes always asked Casey and me about how our day had gone and what we'd done at school, and they encouraged us to talk about things we cared about. For some reason they seemed to believe that children might actually be people, and not just small, annoying house pets."

Michael paused while a slight laugh rippled through the crowd. "A while back," he went on, more slowly now, "our families grew apart. Many of you know about this, and now isn't the time to go into it, but let's just say that I'm full of regret. Because my parents and I loved the Stowe family with all our hearts. And that never stopped, despite what went on between us. And it never will." He had to pause again at this moment, wiping at his eyes before continuing. "I guess no one understands why things happen in life," he said in a quieter voice. "We all just marvel at everything, amazed by it, or angry, or sad, depending on the circumstance. But I'd like to add something." He stopped again. "A long, long time ago, when I was a little kid, my parents and Casey's parents tore down the hedge that separated our houses. And then they built a fountain with angels in the middle of the yard. They told us that the angels were supposed to look like me and Casey. But now, whenever I see that fountain, I know that I'm going to think about Eleanor and Warren Stowe, two angels I was privileged enough to get to know."

Christmas came late that year. The funeral was held on December 26, and the Beckets had decided, since Casey was still a live-in guest at their house, that it would only be appropriate to postpone the exchange of presents for a week. And so it was on New Year's Eve that the Becket family and Casey gathered in the living room.

"I'm afraid I haven't gotten anything for anyone,"

Casey said when she walked in and saw the colorful pile of presents in the middle of the floor and the bottle of champagne on a tray on the coffee table.

"Of course not," Janice Becket said. "Nobody would expect you to. But Tom and I just thought it might be a nice way to celebrate the start of a new year."

"Happy New Year," Tom said quietly, handing a glass of champagne to Casey and raising a glass of his own.

"I don't know what to say—" Casey began.

"Say 'Happy New Year,'" said Michael, standing up from the couch and raising his glass to her.

She smiled. "Happy New Year," she said. "It couldn't be any worse than the old year," she added, and then everyone laughed a little.

There was a dinner lit with candles that night, and the smells of sage and pine perfuming the Becket house, and presents everywhere. They had given Casey a sky blue cashmere sweater, ridiculously expensive, she thought, and yet its softness and extravagance actually cheered her a little.

"This is exactly what I needed," Casey said afterward, leaning back in her chair. "Not just this beautiful sweater. This whole evening. Thank you so much. It's made it easier to come to a decision about something I've been struggling with for the last day or two." She moved her champagne glass from one hand to the other, then let go. "I think it's time for me to go home."

Janice put down her glass. "Are you sure?" she said. "You know you're welcome to stay here as long as you'd like."

"I do know that," Casey said. "And no, I'm not sure. It's going to be difficult. Horrible, I guess. There will be things to go through. My parents' things." She shuddered and shook her head, and her eyes filled at the thought of it. "But it's what I have to do, and putting it off is only making it worse. Besides," Casey went on, "if it gets to be too much for me, I know where to go."

The next morning, she returned to her house, letting herself in to the stillness and walking through the rooms like a visitor to some historical home that's been turned into a museum. The lives that had been lived here, the meals eaten, the bedtime stories told, and how it was all lost now—this might have been overwhelming for her, but Casey forced herself not to think about any of it, or at least as little as possible. And when she couldn't *not* think about it, when it was too much for her, she simply sat down wherever she was, reached for the tissue box she carried with her from room to room, and cried. Then, after a while, she would pick herself up off the floor and go back to packing up her parents' belongings, folding clothes into boxes that would go to the Salvation Army.

It was while she was cleaning out her mother's closet that she found the wedding dress.

There it was, the dress Casey had been wearing the day Will Combray had jilted her. After the guests had gone home that afternoon, Casey had sat in her bedroom and wept, and at some point, she vaguely recalled, her mother had helped her take off the dress, her hands working to loosen each seed-pearl button from its loophole. Casey hadn't known what had become of the dress, and she hadn't wanted to ask. But here was what had become of it: Her mother had packed it in plastic and hung it in the back of her own closet, in a place where Casey would never have to find it and be reminded.

Gently, she lifted it now. She held the dress in her

arms and looked down at it, saw the delicate lace beneath the sheet of plastic. For a moment, she indulged in a memory of Will embracing her, telling her how beautiful she was. Will with his shirt off, his tanned shoulders and chest, his jeans low on his hips, his gorgeous dark eyes.

Enough, she told herself. Quickly, Casey took the wedding dress and walked upstairs. She pulled open the hatch that led to the attic, and she climbed the ladder. Then she walked across the creaking attic floor to an old armoire that had once belonged to her grandmother, and she hung the wedding dress inside it. Here it would stay, she thought, perhaps forever. Then she left the attic quickly, hurrying down the ladder, letting the hatch close behind her, and not looking back.

Casey stayed in her parents' house for several days, cleaning and dusting and preparing it, though for what? She had nowhere else to go and nothing to do, and she felt a kind of emotional flatness that made it impossible for her to plan the future or even feel any excitement about anything. Still, she knew she had pulled herself together once before, and even though the circumstances now were different, and far worse, she had to believe she would be able to do so again. It was like falling in love with Will, she told herself, or falling out of love with Will: She had no choice.

One morning, the doorbell rang, and Casey was surprised to see that it was Michael.

"Can I come in?" he asked, and she nodded, pulling the door wide.

"How have things been?" he said.

She shrugged.

"Right," he said. "How else *could* they be?"

"Come on into the kitchen, Michael," she said, but he shook his head.

"I can't stay," he said. They stood awkwardly in the front hallway for a moment. He seemed to want to say something to her but couldn't bring himself to. Finally, Michael just started to speak. "Casey," he said, "I don't think you should be here any longer. It's not good for you all alone in this house now. You'll just turn into some kind of . . ." Michael's voice trailed off.

"Into what?" she wanted to know.

"Into some kind of person you're not," he said. "Into someone hard. Someone depressed and bitter and sad. Someone without a life. And you deserve better than that."

"So what exactly do you suggest?" she said. "You want to turn back the hands of time so that Will Combray never walked out on me and my parents' car never crashed into that tree? You want to make everything sweet and perfect and back to the way it was, is that it?" She knew how angry she sounded, but she couldn't help herself. "I'm sorry," she said. "I didn't mean it to come out like that."

"Don't be sorry," he said, waving away her apology. "If you can't talk to me like that, who can you talk to?"

He was right. Michael was absolutely right. Casey realized that if it were anyone else standing in the front hall of her house right now—either of Michael's parents, or some aunt or uncle—she wouldn't be speaking like this. This was the way, she understood, you could talk only to a close friend.

Michael took a step toward her now. "I wish more than anything that I could turn back the hands of time," he said evenly. "But I know that's not possible. What I'm suggesting is something different from that."

"Oh?" she said.

"I have to go back to Rhode Island tomorrow. Come with me," he said impulsively. "Don't you have some money from your folks? I could set you up in an inexpensive hotel near the campus. Nothing fancy, but you'd be around people your own age, interesting people, students of all kinds, and you could slowly get back on your feet. I know that you and I aren't really friends anymore, but I still care about you. And I know you can't stay here, Casey, living in the past. I've seen what happens to people who do that. They dry up. They never grow. And I don't want that to happen to you."

She tried to think of some counterargument, but she couldn't, because she knew that Michael was right. There was nothing for her here anymore, except for the ghosts of two parents who had loved her and of a man who she only thought had loved her. It was time to leave.

The next morning, Casey let Michael drive her up to Providence, Rhode Island, where he rented a room for her in a local hotel called the College Gate—nothing fancy, but not remotely seedy, either. Just an old-fashioned, clean room with a four-poster bed, a sink, and a pattern of yellow roses winding down the wallpaper. Michael himself lived in a brick dormitory nearby with a roommate who made gigantic sculptures out of wire and who liked to stay up late into the night, debating Michael about who were the most important artists of the twentieth century.

On their first evening in Rhode Island, Casey went with Michael to a student hangout called The Basket. Together they sat on beanbag chairs and drank beers from a keg and ate little fragments of chips from a bowl that was being passed around. Michael's college friends were so different from the people they had known back in Longwood Falls. They were artistic, daring—more like Will than Michael, she thought to herself.

"So, Casey," said one of the friends, an overweight painter named Cecil, as they all sat in the musty darkness of The Basket, "what are you planning on doing with yourself? Going to school? Getting a job? *Anything?*"

Casey didn't know what to say, and she felt herself flush deeply. It was Michael who spoke up for her. "Casey's in transition," he said, which somehow was the truth, and which silenced Cecil. Casey shot Michael a grateful look. As always, he knew what to do and say.

Night after night, they went to The Basket with his friends, and during the day, when Michael was in classes, Casey walked around Providence, admiring the old brownstones on beautiful, cobblestoned Benefit Street and going into little antiquarian bookstores and art galleries, looking and looking. She had inherited some money from her parents, and she knew she could live this way for a while. In the evening, Michael would pick her up at the College Gate and they would go out to a coffee shop for dinner, where they would sit and talk together before heading over to The Basket to join his friends.

It was, she realized, a little like the old days, when they spent all their time together and couldn't get enough of what the other had to say. Michael wasn't afraid to talk about painful subjects, including her parents and even Will. He was the only person who knew almost everything there was to know about her. He had known her parents better than anyone outside the Stowe family. He also knew how much Will had meant to her and how she still grieved for him. It must have been painful for Michael to discuss Will but, if so, he never showed it.

"The thing about Will," she told Michael late one afternoon over a cup of bitter coffee with flecks of cream floating in it, "is that he seemed so sure he wanted to marry me. That's what I don't understand."

"People can seem sure," said Michael, "but in other ways be very unsure. The inside of a person isn't always represented by the outside."

"I just wonder what's happened to him," she said. "Whether he's all right."

"I'm sure he's fine," Michael said tightly. "Types like him always are."

"He's not a type, he's a person," she corrected. "A person who I thought I understood. But apparently I was wrong," she added.

"I wonder," said Michael, "if we ever really understand one another. I don't mean you and me in particular, but anybody and anybody else. Sometimes I think we're always just peering in through the windows."

"Do you feel that way about me?" Casey asked quietly.

He thought about it for a moment, stirring his cof-
fee, and then he nodded. "Yes, I guess I do," he said.
"Because I never thought you'd go for someone like
Will Combray."

"You don't even know him," said Casey. She
sighed. "Then again, neither do I."

They sat together as the afternoon wore on, and
then they left the diner and went for a walk through
town. Sometimes she fantasized that they would
run into Will on one of their walks, and that by coin-
cidence he would be living right here in Providence—
which in fact wasn't an entirely improbable place for
him to have landed. He would see Casey and regret
what he'd done. He would return to her sheepishly,
like a child who has done something bad and now
needs to confess. Would she take him back? Of course
she would. That was how pathetic she was, she
thought to herself: that she would actually take back
the man who had embarrassed her in front of her family and friends, who had caused her to lose her center
of gravity and her sense of self so completely.

"Michael?" she said now, stopping on the sidewalk down the block from The Basket. "I want to ask
you something."

The Fountain

He stopped and turned toward her.

"Why have you done all of this for me?" she said.

"Done what?" he asked. The streetlight was shining down on him, illuminating the line of his cheekbones, the dark shimmer of his eyes.

"Everything," she said.

"It wasn't a choice," he said quietly, turning his face away.

"What do you mean?"

"You'd have done the same thing for me if the situation were reversed."

"I really love you, you know," Casey blurted out then, before she had a chance to think about what she was saying.

Michael turned back to her and looked at her for a long moment, as though considering something, then looked away again, then back at her once more. And then he said, "Casey?" His voice was soft and hoarse.

"Yes?" she said.

"I love you, too." He took a breath. "Look, I know that the love you feel for me is different from the love I feel for you. But that doesn't matter to me. So what I want to know is whether you'd consider . . ."

He broke off in the middle of the sentence, as though unsure of whether to go on. "Oh, this is total insanity," he said. "I must be the biggest jerk in the world to ask you this, because I'm sure I already know the answer, but I have to plunge ahead and ask it anyway." He took a deep, ragged breath. "Do you think you'd consider marrying me?" Before she could absorb the question, he rushed ahead. "I know we're still young and my parents will think we're out of our minds, but I don't really care. All the loss you've suffered—you can't absorb it on your own. It's not possible. And me: I've loved you my entire life. I've wanted to marry you ever since . . . well, ever since the day I let you help me build that robot."

"With pineapple cans," she said quietly.

"Yes," he said. "With pineapple cans." He paused. "I swear I would take care of you," he said. "We'd take care of each other, the way husbands and wives are supposed to. It wouldn't be anything like what you had with Will; I can't pretend that it would be. I know that you think of me as your friend primarily, and that's the way you'll always think of me. But there are worse things than that, aren't there? I know we could have a real life together, and I promise I'd never let you get lonely. When you needed someone, I'd be right there. You wouldn't have to waste your whole life thinking about Will Combray all the time"—he said Will's name with distaste—"wondering why he disappeared, where he went, what you did wrong. You'd have your own life, with me. A good one."

Michael's eyes were wet now, and she took his hand in both of hers, just holding it like something precious that's been lost and finally found. And when she did say yes to him, her voice was stronger than it had been since the day Will left.

Chapter
Six

૨ら They were married in August. This time there was no tent, no dress, no music, no fanfare at all. Instead, Casey and Michael were ushered into a small room in City Hall late on a Friday afternoon, where an electric fan hummed in the corner and the justice of the peace glanced at his watch a few times during the brief ceremony. Casey wore a simple skirt with wildflowers on it and a sleeveless blue blouse; Michael wore a white linen shirt and a pair of pressed khakis. Standing there stiffly in Room 405, they looked less like a bride and groom than like two college students who were visiting the registrar about a change in their course load. But this was what they wanted: nothing special, a whisper of a wedding.

Michael's parents stood beside the couple, and though sentiment was kept to a minimum during the recital of vows, Janice Becket couldn't stop herself from crying a little, and then Casey began crying, too. Michael looked at her as the tears slid down her cheeks, and his face softened in that moment. He appeared relieved that she was crying, for it allowed him to think there was unfettered emotion in play in the overheated air of this City Hall office.

Let him think that, Casey thought. There are worse things. It wasn't entirely untrue, but it wasn't true in the way he would have hoped.

Later, in their suite at the Longwood Falls Inn—Casey sitting on the edge of the bed and pulling off her pantyhose while Michael stood loosening his tie—he suddenly said to her, "I liked it when you cried."

"Oh," she said. "I hadn't meant to. It just happened." But she knew she hadn't been crying because she loved him the way he deserved to be loved; she'd cried for more complicated reasons: be-

࿓

cause he was a wonderful man who had never given up on her, because her parents were gone forever and weren't there to see her marry, and, finally, because he was not Will Combray. He was so much better than Will, of course, yet knowing this didn't make it easier. Embarrassed by these thoughts now, Casey stood up from the bed and embraced Michael, burying her head against the clean surface of his shirt.

Casey and Michael Becket spent the beginning of their marriage in a tiny apartment on the top floor of a brownstone on Benefit Street in Providence. He was finishing up art school, and she had transferred to a teachers' program at a small local college. They were happy together in a restrained way, eating meatless dinners to save money and sitting up late at night on a mattress on the floor with an Indian-print blanket stretched across it. Orange crates served as furniture, except for two beautiful pieces that Michael had built at school and brought home, and the walls held nothing but a few Rembrandt and Vermeer prints pinned up with thumbtacks.

Casey and Michael felt both very young and very old all at once: too young, in a way, to have married at a time when no one else they knew had taken such a step; and yet too old in feeling as cautious and practical as they did. They were devoted to each other, but not in the way that newlyweds usually are. Instead, Casey sometimes thought, Michael was the brother she never had. They had shared every experience, had known each other since they were born. When they made love in those early days of marriage, there was a carefulness about Michael's style, as though he were fearful she might break. They never talked about this quality, though surely, Casey thought, Michael must have been aware of it.

"I'm not a china doll!" she considered blurting out to him once when they had finished making love and were lying together on the mattress, a James Taylor record playing softly and scratchily in the background. But when she looked over at him and saw how content he seemed, she said nothing. It was true; there was an imbalance between them. Where he was content, she was both restless and grateful. He was probably the worthiest man she'd ever known; he had taken her at her lowest point and lifted her up. Whenever Casey was reminded of her parents and became upset, Michael would always know the right thing to say. Sometimes he knew enough to say nothing at all but just to let her talk, let her bring up memories of her mother and father until she had wound down.

By the time Casey graduated from college with a degree in elementary education, Michael had taken a job as an apprentice to a furniture maker, and though it paid next to nothing, he was learning a great deal, and he assured Casey that it would pay off in the long run. *The long run*: For her, these words had no meaning. She could only imagine life in the short run, the day-to-dayness of it all, one morning leading to an afternoon, and then to an evening, and a night, and then another morning. This was how a marriage was built, piece by piece. She had no romantic fantasy of two people entwined, aloft; that had died with Will's rejection of her. Still, the short run did somehow keep lengthening, and one day Casey woke up nauseated, leaping out of bed and hurrying to the tiny bathroom to be sick. Michael held her head and brought her ice chips, and though her bout of illness might just as easily have been caused by a stomach bug, both she and Michael knew: Casey was pregnant.

The twins were delivered by cesarean section on a hot night in July, and from the start they were different from each other. Hannah was born with her eyes wide open and staring out at the world, Rachel with her eyes squeezed tightly shut, a physical presentation that would continue to characterize the twins even in those early months: Hannah the curious and game-for-anything baby, Rachel the watchful sibling. Late that summer, the family traveled back to Longwood Falls to finally figure out what to do with Casey's house. For a long time it had remained unlived in, other than the occasional visit by Casey and Michael, or Janice Becket "just to check on things," which essentially meant doing a little dusting and a lot of remembering. In these rooms, long ago, two families had chatted and eaten meals and played Twister; now the rooms were unnaturally silent.

It was time to sell the house, Casey and Michael knew. The money the sale would bring them would be enormously helpful; they could buy their own house in Providence and start a real life there. But this time, when Casey walked back in through the front door of her childhood home on Strawberry Street, she was hit with a surprising rush of nostalgia, so strong it seemed as if there were an intoxicant in the air.

"Whoa," she said, as she stood in the front hall, looking around.

"Whoa what?" asked Michael.

"Just . . . whoa," said Casey. "As in 'Whoa, I can't believe this.' It looks the same but smaller. As if I've grown or something, since I moved out."

"Well, you have," said Michael.

And she had, of course. Michael had returned her to herself, slowly and surely taking care of her until she was less mournful, less full of loss. He had treated her much the way he treated a piece of fine furniture he was restoring: with painstaking affection and attention. And, like his furniture, she shone. So when Casey came back to the house on Strawberry Street, she was no longer the sad young woman for whom the house brought only painful memories. Instead, she seemed to be a different person in a different house. And it was an appealing place, she realized as she walked through the rooms, carrying Hannah in her arms while Michael carried Rachel.

"Look, honey," she told her baby, "here's the bedroom where Mommy grew up. I used to have a crib over here against this wall. And right above it there was a mobile with panda bears hanging from it. I think we still might have that mobile somewhere. . . ."

Casey pictured Rachel and Hannah sleeping in this room, living out the kind of childhood that she had once had herself. Longwood Falls wasn't exactly the most exciting place in the world, and Casey had never expected to come back here to stay, but it was an idea she liked, an idea that suddenly seemed to make perfect sense.

"Michael," she said, turning to him, "I know you're going to be shocked by what I'm about to ask you. But would you consider living here?"

He looked at her, his mouth dropping open slightly. "You're kidding," he said at first. Then, after a moment, "No, you're not kidding. Well, wow, Casey, it never occurred to me to think about that. I mean, the last time we were here, you couldn't wait to get away. But now I guess things are different— the kids, and your teaching degree and everything." He shook his head slowly. "My parents would be out of their minds with happiness, of course," he added. "Though we shouldn't let that stop us."

The advantages to moving into the house were obvious. Number 11 Strawberry Street would be perfect for the children, with its double-wide backyard and ready supply of grandparents next door at Number 9. Still, something about the situation nagged at Casey. It wasn't leaving Providence; while they'd made good friends there, the small New England city had always felt like a stopping-off place on the way to somewhere else. It had never occurred to Casey that the "somewhere else" would be the place she knew better than any place else on Earth. But then again, it had never occurred to Casey that the things that had happened to her would have happened to her. When Michael took her away from Longwood Falls, he had pretty much saved her life. And now, having been saved, she was ready to return.

"It's not going to be the same," she said to Michael the night before they left their tiny apartment in Rhode Island to move back home.

"Yeah, I know." Michael didn't look up from a

cardboard box of pots and pans he was trying to press closed. "The kids will have lots more room, for one," he went on. "And they're really going to need it."

"I don't mean the same as Providence," she said. At the moment, the entire contents of their lives were stacked before them in boxes in the living room; tomorrow all this would be scattered throughout the house she had grown up in. Casey hugged herself against a sudden chill. "I mean, the same as it used to be when we were growing up."

He looked at her. "Oh. Of course not." Michael straightened up from the box. "It'll never be the same without your parents there, you mean."

"No, I don't mean just that," she said. "I do mean that, and I don't."

"Look, you're right," he said, coming over and putting his arms around her. "It will never be what it was. But all that means," he went on, "is that we'll just have to make it something else. You know, our own."

And so they did. Within days of moving back, Michael found a job with an antique furniture workshop in town, the House of Stanton, where he executed simple repairs and helped out with the shop's more elaborate restoration projects. Casey was planning on looking for a teaching job as soon as the twins were old enough (thanks to a grandmotherly offer from Janice Becket to watch them during the afternoons), but what happened instead was that Casey became pregnant again, and so going back to work would have to be put off a bit longer.

Alex was born six weeks early, a red baby the size of a small frying chicken who didn't sleep through the night until he was five months old, and so the dominant theme in the household, for a long time, was exhaustion. Once, in the early hours of the morning when Casey sat in a rocking chair in the corner of the room nursing the baby, and Michael struggled to stay awake in the bed to keep her company, they began to list all the things they wanted to do with their lives.

"Have my own furniture studio," Michael said.

"Have my own class to teach," said Casey.

"Live long enough to see all our kids get married," said Michael with a big yawn, which was a startling idea to Casey as she held Alex against her breast. How could this sweet-smelling baby, with the soft spot on his head and the tiny starfish hands, possibly grow up and leave home one day? More to the point, how could she ever let him? But that was what children do, eventually—leave. Wasn't that what Casey had been trying to do with Will Combray, she realized as she nursed her baby: leave the safety of her parents' world? Once in a while, thoughts about Will came drifting down like a surprise snowfall—even now, in this beatific moment with her son and her husband, when the idea of Will Combray should have been far, far away from the safe confines of this room. But it wasn't; that idea had returned again, making her recall how, when she was a teenage girl in love with Will, all she had wanted was to be heading somewhere—it hardly mattered where. All that mattered was how far and how fast she could go.

But that effort had exhausted her and nearly destroyed her, and now Casey wanted nothing more than to stay perfectly still. To make time stop. To spend forever inhaling the scent of her baby son after a bath and playing peekaboo with her twin daughters. Sometimes she and Michael planted the three children on the bed between them, the five Beckets in their pajamas on the poppy-flower sheets in the morning sunlight, and Casey watched the children moving and touching one another, creating their own society.

From the outside, Casey knew, this life that she and Michael had constructed for themselves might look unexciting. Unexciting and *small*. It would have looked that way to her, too, in passing, from the back of Will's motorcycle. But from the inside, their life was merely compact. It was manageable, and it was calm, and it held few surprises. It was, in short, everything that Casey now craved. For when your entire existence is shaken up and the rug is pulled out from under you, sometimes all you want in the end is a similar rug.

For a long time, life on Strawberry Street was mostly satisfying. When the children were finally old enough, Casey took a job teaching at the Longwood Falls Middle School—the same school she and Michael had attended long ago. The halls felt narrower, of course, but they still smelled the same: of pencil shavings, and gym sweat, and that strange schoolhouse fragrance she couldn't name but had never forgotten. Teaching was everything Casey had hoped for, and sometimes, as she stood at the blackboard writing something down with a piece of chalk that, due to her enthusiasm, had been whittled down to the size of a raisin, she remembered her old piano teacher, Dorian Bradley, who had inspired her to become a teacher, and Casey hoped that she might be serving as some sort of inspiration for one of *her* students.

It was difficult being away from her own children, though they were happily ensconced, first in a cooperative nursery school and then, later, in kindergarten at Longwood Falls Primary. Janice Becket often said that the sight of her grandchildren running around the backyard reminded her of Casey and Michael when they were kids, but nobody would have mistaken Hannah, Rachel, and Alex for next-door neighbors or the best of friends. The three of them were siblings through and through.

"Stop following me!" Casey heard Hannah shrieking once when she was five and Alex four, and she looked up from the romaine lettuce she was washing in the kitchen sink to see her daughter storming off across the lawn, away from the uncomprehending Alex.

"Hannah!" Casey dutifully called out through the

screen. "Be nice to your brother!" But she understood Hannah's frustration: Already Alex was tagging along behind her, calling Hannah's name, going back for more. They weren't like her and Michael as kids at all, Casey thought then; they were like her and Michael as teenagers, before Will.

She and Michael hardly ever talked about Will Combray anymore. In the beginning, when Michael had installed Casey in a room in the College Gate Hotel in Providence, they had talked frankly about what Will had meant to her. Then, in the early days of her marriage to Michael, they'd continued to talk about him from time to time. Sometimes, Casey had noticed that Michael looked uncomfortable when she spoke of Will, that he tapped his fingers on the table or played with the edge of a cuff.

Once, when the children were still in the early grades, the family went out for dinner to The Granary to sample its recently introduced under-age-twelve menu. Rachel and Hannah had ordered "The Zebra" (spaghetti and meatballs) and Alex "The Lion" (a grilled cheese sandwich). Casey realized, as she picked up her fork to eat her chicken salad, that she had not set foot in this restaurant since the night Will took her here.

She must have gotten that faraway, "Don't mind me, I'm thinking of Will again" look, for Michael picked up on it right away. "What is it?" he asked her.

"Nothing," she said.

"You look preoccupied," he persisted.

"It's just . . ." Casey began. "This place."

Michael paused, and then his face flushed slightly. "Oh, that's right," he said. "This is where you went with him, right?"

"Right," she said with a little laugh that she hoped he'd join. He didn't. Though plenty of time had passed and Will Combray was not relevant in any way, Michael still didn't hide how he felt about him. "If I'd known, I would have suggested somewhere else," he said.

"Oh, come on," Casey said, trying to make light of it. "Where else in town can the children eat zebra? And besides, Will was a million years ago. You don't really mind, Michael, do you?"

"Mind what?" Michael asked evenly, not taking his eyes from her as he drank his glass of beer.

174

The Fountain

~~

"Mind that about a million years ago, I came here with Will," said Casey.

"Mommy, who's Will?" asked Alex, looking up from his sandwich. "Is it Will Shakespeare?"

"William Shakespeare," said Rachel with contempt. "And he's been dead for years and years."

"At least a hundred years," added Hannah, trying to be helpful.

"Will, Will, Will," sang Alex. "Will makes me ill."

"Me, too," said Michael quietly, with a hard smile.

"Well, then," said Casey, "I won't mention him again. There's no reason to, anyway."

"You can mention him," said Michael. "Really, it's totally okay. I admit that in the rare moments when you say his name I do feel a twinge, but it's all right. There are worse things in the world than twinges."

But even though Michael insisted it was fine, Casey decided to mention Will as seldom as possible. There was no need, really; in the early years of their marriage, when she was still vulnerable and the wounds were still tender, there *had* been a need—an urgency, as if she had to get it out of her system. But now the desire to talk about Will surfaced only occasionally, and even then quickly passed. Late on a summer day, drifting outside to close the umbrella over the picnic table, Casey might find herself standing by the fountain, idly running her hand along the still surface of the water that had pounded there during a recent rainstorm, and she would think about that moment so many years earlier when she had stood on this very spot, kissing Will on a night much like this one, his hands all over her, his breath on her neck, and Michael had seen them. And then Casey would think, I must go back in the house right this minute and tell Michael—tell him about that memory and how strongly she could feel it to this day, the combination of happiness and hopeless misery she'd experienced in that one piercing moment when Michael confronted her the next morning in her kitchen—because that's what she always thought when she had something that needed saying: I must tell Michael. And then, just as suddenly, Casey would decide that of course she wouldn't tell Michael. She wouldn't tell anyone, because there was nobody to tell. And then Casey would lift her hand out of the fountain water, dry it on her jeans, and drift back inside the house.

The Fountain

ॐ

* * *

One day, when the twins were in junior high school, they were fooling around in the attic on a drizzly weekend afternoon and found the wedding dress their mother had hung in an armoire many years earlier. It wasn't as if Casey had been hiding it, really. The dress had been hanging in plain sight for years—or would have been, if anyone had bothered to pull down the ladder leading to the attic and then elbow aside the garment bags in the old armoire.

"Mom!" Rachel called down to Casey. "Come up here for a sec!"

"Oh, my God," Casey said when she climbed up the ladder and saw what was on display.

"Is this what I think it is?" Hannah said, lifting the dress through the front of the bag. But before Casey had a chance to come up with an answer, Hannah went on, "God, Mom, I can't believe you got married at City Hall and you still went to all the trouble to have a real wedding gown. I never knew that."

Although Casey and Michael had always answered their children's questions about their wedding day truthfully—saying yes, the wedding was small and rather businesslike, given its locale, and the honeymoon, if you could call it that, was incredibly brief—they'd never felt the need to volunteer the details of the drama that preceded it. Will Combray didn't exist in the imaginations of her children. Casey wondered now if the time had come to tell them that before she'd married Michael, she'd been passionately in love with and engaged to—and finally jilted by—another man. But Casey was spared having to decide what to say by the kind of absolute self-absorption that comes so easily to teenagers.

"When *I* get married," Hannah was saying, already losing interest in Casey's past, "I know just what I want. No City Hall ceremony for me—I mean, no offense, Mom, but I want a real wedding. The kind that everybody always remembers forever. My wedding is going to be held at the seashore, and there will be tons of people, and a really awesome reggae band playing, and there will be a vanilla cake with silver decorations, and champagne and dancing. And we'll recite these really cool poems that we write ourselves, and then everybody will jump into the water and go swimming."

"Weddings aren't everything," Casey said carefully. "They're important. But what really matters isn't how two people begin their life together, it's how they spend it."

"*Lots* of dancing," Rachel put in, oblivious. "To really, really great music. And loud, too. House music. Not that old, slow stuff you guys like."

Casey nearly laughed at how thoroughly her daughters weren't listening to her. But who could blame them? When Casey was their age, she didn't listen to her mother, either. If Casey had in fact confided in her daughters about Will, would they even have believed that image of their still-youthful but predictable schoolteacher mother, some twenty years earlier, riding on the back of a motorcycle, her hair flowing out behind her? Would they have believed the image of the man their mother had loved: moody, unruly Will, who was so different from their father?

Now it was Hannah and Rachel's turn to begin bringing boys to the house, and sometimes Casey would glimpse in a swagger or a half-smirk something that reminded her of Will. These kinds of boys were always exciting to girls, because they seemed slightly out of reach, slightly untrappable, and always mysterious. All women, Casey realized, have a

Will Combray in their lives at one time or another. And usually, like Will, they disappear.

"Well, I think the fashion show is over," Casey said after the girls had finished describing their plans for a perfect wedding. Then, trying to keep her emotions safely at bay, Casey carefully tucked the dress back into the garment bag and zipped it up.

Was it really possible that Casey would never see Will again? Once, she hadn't even known to ask such a question of anyone. In those days, she hadn't yet weathered the terrible, aching loss of her parents. She hadn't yet witnessed, in a fractured elbow or a spiking fever, the fragility of her own children. As the years went on, though, she couldn't help wondering, if only in passing, whether that was *it*, as far as she and Will were concerned: a brief, all-consuming period of teenage togetherness, followed by nothing, forever.

Casey had no idea where Will was or what had become of him, but she could imagine him living in someplace cosmopolitan and fast-paced, like New York City. Once a year, Casey took her fifth-grade students on a train trip down along the Hudson River into Manhattan, a dozen boys and girls for whom "the big city" might otherwise have meant Albany. Once in Manhattan, of course, she took them to the usual landmarks, including the Statue of Liberty and the Empire State Building, but she also made sure to teach them how to ride subways, how to use chopsticks and hail a taxi. "I'm not saying you have to like it here," she always informed the kids as she led them through the bazaarlike atmosphere of St. Mark's Place in the chaotic East Village, with its sidewalk displays of jewelry and folk art and vendors selling shish kebab on every corner. "I'm not saying this is better than Longwood Falls—or worse," she would continue. "I just want you to know what some of your options are." And then at some point she would step out of a handsome middle-aged man's path at a Fifty-seventh Street crosswalk, and her heart would leap and she would ask herself: Is that him?

And what if it were? Would she have anything to say to Will now? Or he to her? She had to wonder at such moments whether it might be better to leave the past alone and never see him again. But as she grew older, Casey also found herself asking: What have I got to lose?

Maybe once, a long time ago, it had made sense for her to believe it was best if she went the rest of her life without seeing Will Combray again. But over time it came to seem absurd in some way for two people who once couldn't get enough of each other, who had planned to spend the rest of their lives together, simply to go their separate ways and never look back. Never to find out what had happened to that other person. To care for a time, maybe, and then stop.

Once, while Casey was leading her class through a Fifth Avenue bookstore, one with brass railings in the balcony and wooden ladders on rollers, she asked a clerk, a tall young man with a diamond stud on the tip of his tongue, "Is there a poetry section here?" The clerk led her to an alcove in the back of the store, and while her students whispered about whether a diamond stud on the tip of the tongue would hurt (yes was the consensus), Casey ran a finger along the spines of the books by authors whose last names began with the letter C.

All right, so Will hadn't become a poet.

"Could you tell me where the fiction section is?" Casey asked then, and this time the clerk directed her to the front of the store. But Will Combray wasn't there, either, and he wasn't listed in the giant catalog of books in print that the store kept behind the cash register. Maybe the books of Will Combray were out of print, Casey thought, or maybe the books he'd written had never been published. Or maybe he didn't wind up as a writer but as a painter or as a musician. Maybe he wasn't in America at all; maybe he'd become a professor of philosophy in Paris.

Maybe he was dead.

The thought struck her with a shock. In all the times over the decades that Casey had wondered about whatever had become of Will Combray, this was the first time she could remember considering the possibility that the answer might be: nothing. That he might be no more. She realized now that she'd always just assumed he was out there, some-where; the possibility that he might not be had sim-ply never occurred to her. Which, in a way, made no sense at all, since her own parents had been taken young, in one swift blow. But such was the enduring force of Will's presence in her life that it wasn't until she realized she might never see him again that she understood how deeply she'd always expected that she would.

"Mrs. Becket? Can we go now? Please? Mrs. Becket?" Gregory Kirsch, one of her students, had stationed himself in front of her, trying to get her attention. "Mrs. *Becket*," he said again, this time with enough insistence that Casey finally recognized herself in the name she'd taken, nearly twenty years earlier, from her husband.

Chapter
Seven

❧

❧ The decision to telephone Will at the inn on Friday morning was far from spontaneous. Casey had spent much of the previous night going back and forth in her mind over whether she should make the call, and when she finally slept, somewhere in the vicinity of 2:00 A.M., she dreamed of her hand hovering like a pale bird over the surface of a telephone. Michael was an early riser, and by the time Casey woke up, she found that he'd already gone to work, leaving a note on the pillow that said, "C.— Good luck with everything today! Love, M." He was referring, of course, to the busy and frenetic day she was going to have, running last-minute errands for the party and preparing for the arrival of the twins from Ithaca by bus, and not to the fact that she might or might not be calling Will Combray. But if she did call him, she thought as she read Michael's note, luck was indeed exactly what she'd need.

Casey lay in bed for a few minutes, blinking and getting her bearings. Don't call him, she thought. Let it go. Drop it like a hot potato—a phrase her mother had often used. If she chose not to call him, then there would be a logical arc to their entire relationship: She had loved him when he was young and been hurt by him; then she had seen him again when he was not so young and shared a quick, intense moment of sensation with him for which she would never have reason to feel guilt. *End of story.*

But Casey also understood, as she lingered in the warm, rumpled bed a little while longer, that she didn't want this to be the end of the story; she wasn't ready for such closure. Yesterday, Will had said it would be up to her whether to call. He hadn't been pushy or cocky about it, the way he'd once been, long ago, when he'd leaned against the side of the Savings and Loan Building downtown and talked to

⤳

her in a way no one ever had before. No, the new Will Combray—the fully grown version—was chastened and regretful, though unmistakably still full of feeling toward her. He'd mellowed, the way all people did as they got older. He was slower, softer-spoken, more melancholy to be sure. If she met this man now—as the father of a student walking into her classroom for a parent-teacher conference, for instance—she might momentarily note in some reflexive way that he was attractive, but that would be the end of it. Why would there be anything more? Her marriage was sound and secure and loving, and Casey had never done anything to threaten it. The sight of someone like Will Combray walking into her life didn't hold any particular appeal for her. The difference now, however, was that Will wasn't someone *like* Will Combray; he *was* Will Combray. And what drew Casey to Will was her knowledge of who he'd been, that teenage boy who must still be alive, somewhere inside. That's the person she's always wondered about: What had become of *him*?

Casey leaned across the bed, grazing the pillow where Michael had recently slept, and picked up the telephone receiver. Will answered abruptly on the

first ring, as if he'd been staring at the phone, waiting for her call, and for a moment what seemed to be
his eagerness almost frightened her into hanging up.

"This is Casey," she said, and she couldn't be
sure, but it sounded as though Will let out a breath
of relief.

"Good," he said simply. "I'm glad."

"I just thought I'd call," she said, not knowing
what else to say.

"I was sitting here in my room with a cup of really
bad coffee," he said. The sound of Will Combray's
rough-edged, untried morning voice over the wire
made her listen more closely, seemed to drive her ear
harder against the receiver. "Just sitting here, wondering whether or not you'd call."

"And what did you decide?" she asked.

"I was on the fence," he said.

"Me, too," said Casey.

"I don't mean to be an intrusion or anything,"
Will said. "I know you're very busy. I guess I picked
a bad time to visit."

"Your timing could use a little work, that's true,"
she admitted, and something in her tone reminded
her of the gently teasing way she and Will used to

speak, as if constantly testing each other. But then Casey retreated to her usual mode these days, that of responsible mother and wife, as she rattled off the list of things she had to do today: drive to the tailor's in a nearby town, Cedar Vale, to pick up the pale blue dress she was going to wear to the anniversary party; make a trip to the liquor store and the party supplies store and the florist. It was as if she didn't want him to get the wrong idea about her calling him—though what exactly the right idea was, she couldn't say.

"Well," Will said when she'd finished her recitation, "could you use a little company?"

"You mean go with me on my errands?" she asked. "Why would you want to do that?"

"Just so we could talk," he said.

"I'm warning you, it will be extremely boring," Casey insisted.

"I don't care," Will said. "We could sit on the floor of a hardware store under a display of ball-peen hammers and it would be fine. I just want to have a little time with you, Casey. I'm leaving tomorrow."

So she let him come. This is ridiculous, or at least ridiculously impetuous, she thought as she got dressed in a bottle green blouse, jade earrings, and a fresh pair of jeans and sandals. This is ridiculous, she thought as she buckled herself into the minivan and drove over to pick him up at the Longwood Falls Inn—the place where she and Michael had spent their honeymoon night.

And then there he was, sitting on a bench outside the pretty, gabled facade of the hotel, and suddenly it didn't seem so ridiculous. In her mind, over the years he had grown into a figure larger than life: Will Combray, The Man Who Mysteriously Dumped Me on My Wedding Day. But now here he was, one more distracted-looking person at the side of the road, an anonymous man in a royal blue shirt and khaki pants, whose fingers wouldn't stop drumming against the surface of the bench. And here, for that matter, she was: no longer a late-1970s teenager with a wild spray of blond hair, and patchouli perfume dabbed onto her wrists and neck, and Swedish clogs on her feet, but instead a contemporary, forty-year-old, married grade-school teacher and mother of three, piloting an undeniably mom-like, suburban van.

The Fountain

✣

She pulled up the circular drive of the inn, leaned across the front seat, and swung the door wide for Will. He smiled and climbed in slowly, cautiously, like someone who'd never ridden in a minivan before. And perhaps he hadn't. It seemed more likely to Casey that Will's life took him in and out of taxis and town cars and the occasional sport utility vehicle.

"Hi," she said.

"Hello," he answered.

Good, she thought: no "Vanilla." Nothing flirtatious at all. Just two old friends going for a drive.

They rode in silence for a while. Then, when they did start talking, it was just polite chatter. Casey told Will about some of the changes in the town over the two decades since he'd lived here, pointing out buildings that had sprouted in previously empty fields or lots, and the ghosts of other buildings that had long ago been torn down to make way for a medical arts complex or a highway.

"Remember the Cottonwood Dairy Market?" she asked him.

He nodded. "Sure. I used to buy myself little containers of milk and powdered-sugar doughnuts there when I lived at the boardinghouse. Mrs. Lynchley always complained that I left a trail of powdered sugar on her rug."

"It's a day care center now," said Casey.

"Oh," said Will softly. "And what about the boardinghouse itself?"

"I went by it just a couple of months ago," Casey said casually, "and there was a 'For Sale' sign up."

"I remember that place very well," said Will in a strangely tight voice, and she knew he was thinking about what had happened there between the two of them. Which she was thinking about, too, now, though trying not to.

"Let's go see it," Will suddenly said. "If you wouldn't mind. We could just swing by, before going off to Cedar Vale to get that dress of yours."

Casey hesitated. What harm could it do? she asked herself, and yet even the idea of visiting this place—this charged place—with the man she had made love to there seemed dangerous. But it was dangerous only in her mind, she knew, in her mind that held on to images forever, never letting them go, never letting them lose their resonance. It wasn't dangerous in reality, she decided, because she was in charge, not he. Because she was no longer a nineteen-year-old who, around Will, felt as if she had no choice. She nodded and suddenly turned off the highway, looping back around to the outskirts of Longwood Falls, past the rows of scrub pines and the recycling plant and the school-bus yard, with its row after row of bright yellow buses hibernating until September, and then finally she reached the place where the boardinghouse still stood.

The white wooden building was set back from the unmarked road. Casey pictured Mrs. Lynchley standing in the doorway and unabashedly watching as Casey and Will climbed the stairs together to his room. Mrs. Lynchley had most likely been dead for many, many years, and whoever owned the place now hadn't had any luck in selling it yet, for the FOR SALE sign was still tilted in a patch of earth by the front steps.

"God, get a load of this place," Will said quietly. "I feel like we've stepped into a time warp."

"We have," said Casey, and she shut off the engine of the van. "Want to look around?" she asked, trying to seem as though she herself was only vaguely drawn in by the sight of this sagging, abandoned property.

"Okay," he answered, as if the thought had just occurred to him, too.

And so they climbed out of the van and walked up to the porch, peering in through dark, cloudy windows. Casey could see that the building was empty now, all the charmless thrift-store furniture long ago removed. Will tried the front door, and the knob turned easily.

"Would you look at that," he said, shaking his head in surprise. "Small-town life." Then he stepped inside, followed tentatively by Casey. Together they walked through the front room, their shoes thudding hollowly on the floorboards. They stopped in the center of the room and simply stood there, in the stale, unmoving air, taking in the splintered woodwork and the paint peeling in curlicues.

"Well, it never was much to look at, even back then," Will said.

Casey smiled.

"Want to go up?" he asked her after a moment. "Just to see?"

The Fountain

᠅

"Do you think it's safe?" Casey said, looking at the thin boards of the steps leading to the second floor.

"One way to find out," Will said.

And so they set off on a walking tour of their past, just the two of them. It was a frightening thing to do—and not just because of rickety floorboards—but it was also too exciting to pass up. Having come this far, how could Casey possibly turn back? This was the way she used to operate when she was young, she realized—trying to make decisions based on whether the excitement outweighed the danger or the other way around. When Will had first burst into her life, it hadn't taken much for her to realize that the excitement he aroused in her was too great to ignore, even if the danger in him was real.

She held on to the shaky banister now as they ascended the steps together, climbing to the second floor, where Will's rented room had been. The hallway was dark, with a broken bulb hanging from a cord and an unlit exit sign on the far wall. The doors that lined the hallway were open, offering views into the identically tiny, empty rooms. Casey tried not to look, as if the lives that had passed there were tiny and empty too, and, therefore, hers and Will's, by some sort of mathematical property she probably could have explained to her fifth graders. Finally they arrived at Will's room, the last one on the left-hand side. The door was flung wide, revealing the small space that had once held a dresser and, of course, a lumpy, iron-railed bed.

Casey and Will hesitated on the threshold, then stepped inside. The only remnant of their past was the round mirror that for some reason had been left to hang on the wall above the place where the dresser had stood. In the mottled, gunmetal-colored glass, Casey could see both of their reflections, the startling, older incarnations of two teenagers who had made love in this very room, over and over, holding each other tightly. In the mirror she saw Will's sand-colored hair with the silver in it, and the collar of his good blue shirt; she saw her own delicate, hesitant, middle-aged self with the jade earrings slightly showing through beneath the sheaf of blond hair. Who *were* these people? Whoever they were, they were certainly far removed from the teenagers who had once undressed together in this room, unbuttoning each other's clothes and enjoying the exhilaration of being young and in love and lying in bed together in the middle of the day. You could never reclaim those selves; they had disappeared forever, like Casey's wild hair and Will Combray's swagger.

"What happened to us?" she asked him now, looking away from the mirror image of him and instead at the real thing.

Will forced a smile. "We went away," he said in a hoarse voice.

"No," Casey said suddenly, not willing to let the moment turn sentimental. "You went away."

Will ducked his head down in a half nod. "I went away," he agreed. For a few seconds, he put his hands in his pockets and just gazed out the dirty window at the pines that were tipped with light. Then, finally, he spoke again, in a voice that was almost unrecognizable. "I'm so sorry," he said. "So very sorry. I can't begin to tell you."

She nodded; that was all she would give him for now: a nod. Once, he had broken her heart. He had *wrenched* her; he had caused her to stay inside her bedroom, ashamed and crying and always wondering why it had happened. He had embarrassed her in front of everyone she knew; he had destroyed her, at least for a while. And then, a few months later, when her parents had been killed, he hadn't been there for her. He had changed her life: for better or for worse was beside the point and impossible to say, anyway. But altered it, once and always, in uncountable, unimaginable, and forever unknowable ways. When she thought of it all now, in this concentrated moment, she felt as though it might knock her over with its full force. She closed her eyes, pressing her fingers in a steeple to her face. Then she opened her eyes again and asked him, "Why?"

"Why?" he said.

"Yes. Why. You said yesterday that you'd come back here to find yourself, to get back to the point in your life when everything started to fall apart. This seems like a good place to start. So tell me: Why did it happen like that?"

Casey was aware that her voice, in this room with no furniture or carpeting to absorb sound, had a hollow staginess to it, and she was almost sorry she'd asked him the exact question she'd always wanted to ask him, for she knew it made her seem vulnerable. But here he was—he'd landed on her doorstep out of nowhere—so why shouldn't she ask him what she had wanted to know all along: Was it her? Was that why he left? Was it something she had done or not done? *Why did he leave her?*

"I left because I was weak," he began. "It was true that I'd been traveling around trying to get experience and be a writer, but I didn't know jack about the world. I grew up in a logging camp, remember. It was all work, day and night. You were measured only by how many trees you'd cut down. The men had to be a certain way, full of muscle, and bragging about their exploits. My father was like that, certainly, and he expected me to be like that, too. But of course I couldn't be like him at all, so instead I developed this *attitude*—the Will Combray Special— but really, I was just as wide-eyed as you were. Truthfully, I didn't know what the hell I was doing. You were the first person I'd ever met who offered me something stable—a home, a whole world that was totally new to me. We were going to have all of that eventually, after we got sick of traveling around on my bike, remember?"

"Oh, yes," she said softly.

"And it's not that I didn't want it, Casey," Will

said. "I wanted it more than anything. But there was this little voice in me that kept popping up like my conscience or something, like Jiminy Cricket, and telling me, *You don't deserve this girl. Get the hell out of here.* I tried to ignore it as long as I could, but it kept coming back." He paused for a moment. "The night before our wedding," Will continued, "I was lying in this crummy little room, and my conscience paid me a last visit, reminding me that you were too good for me, that I wasn't up to dealing with all the responsibilities I'd have if I got married the next day, that I should get out now before I totally screwed up two people's lives, instead of just my own." Will took a deep breath, and then he seemed to think for a while, and then he shrugged. "So I left."

"Without telling me," Casey said, astonished to feel the full freight of her anger returning. She had not felt this in many years, and it came as a shock. She could even almost feel the material of her wedding dress against her now, the watered silk and the seed-pearl buttons that had taken so long to button up and, a little later, to unbutton while she was crying and the guests were all beating a hasty, flustered retreat back across the lawn and into the street, their car keys already in their hands. If Will had come back a few days later and explained why he hadn't gone through with the wedding, she would have been able to confront him, scream at him, and get over him. But he hadn't come back, and she'd never had a chance to confront him until now. And now, the pretty, composed, forty-year-old teacher he'd come to see had morphed back into her earlier self. She was nineteen years old and furious. She hated him, this man who himself had suddenly morphed into his own nineteen-year-old self.

"How could you," she said quietly, and it wasn't a question. Casey came forward, felt herself starting to shake, a muscle twitching in her left eye. Without even thinking, she gave him a shove right on his chest, pushing him with surprising power. He staggered backward, and his arms windmilled a little, catching himself from falling. Shocked at what she'd done, Casey turned and started to walk toward the door.

"Casey, wait," said Will. "Wait."

He loped forward and touched her shoulder. As

she turned around and looked at him then, she saw that he was crying, the tears coming hard down his face. "I love you, you know," he said.

Casey stopped. The muscle in her eye still twitched; she felt her own heartbeat also, the two rhythms slightly off, competing with each other like the bass line coming from amplifiers in two different rooms. "You do not," she told him.

"I do," said Will. "I love you, and I've always loved you. It never stopped, never."

"Don't—" she said, putting up a hand to silence him. "Just don't."

"Why?" he said. "Because you don't feel it? Because you feel nothing for me?"

"Because I'm married," Casey said, "because tomorrow is my twentieth wedding anniversary. Because I have a *life* here, Will, and you can't just burst into it like this. You just can't."

"Haven't you ever wondered 'what if?'" he asked her.

"Of course I have," Casey said, "but it's totally irrelevant."

"What if?" he pressed. "What if I'd stayed here and married you? What if it was *our* wedding anniversary we were celebrating tomorrow?" He took a breath. "If I could go back, I would. And I'd ask you to marry me in this room again"—Will gestured broadly with his arms, encompassing the small, barren space—"and this time I'd show up." He took a cautious step, moving closer to her.

Casey could have pushed him away again; it would have been so easy to do that. She could have pushed him away and gone out to her van, as she should have, and left him alone with his boarding-house and its ghosts and no way to get back home.

Instead, she stood perfectly still. So did he. They were facing each other like partners in a formal dance, a gavotte. They just stood there for a moment, as if waiting for the music to begin.

And then it did. Will reached up, touching her neck with his hand, lifting the hair that hung there, making the jade earring swing lightly, like the clapper of a bell, though silent.

"What are you trying to do, Will?" she asked him. "Are you trying to torment me? Because you've always known how to do that, haven't you?"

"Torment you?" he said quietly, and he shook his head. "Oh, Casey," he said, "that's the last thing I'd want to do." He waited a moment. "I came back to town for the reasons I told you. Because my second wife had left me, and I needed to find out where everything went bad. Because I was lost. But the thing is," he continued, "I don't feel lost now. Not at all. I feel good. Better than any single moment since that summer when I walked out of this room without saying good-bye to you. I made a terrible, terrible mistake, Casey. And I don't want to spend the rest of my life saying 'What if?' "

"There's no choice," she said, her voice cracking in the middle.

"But there *is*," he said, and then, as if to prove his point, he leaned forward and bent his head down, planting a kiss on the hollow of her neck. It had once been a place where she loved to be kissed by him; did he remember, after all this time? Yes, she knew, he remembered, and she remembered, too, her body responding to the kiss against all reason. She took his head in her hands. Forgive me, God, she thought, though she wasn't a very religious person, and then she corrected herself: Forgive me, Michael. But even as she thought this, she knew that Michael would never forgive her, and that he would have no reason to. She leaned upward, wanting more of this, wanting Will Combray's mouth on her neck, her mouth, her breast—everywhere that was her. She was horrified at herself, at how quickly she could turn back into the ardent, hopelessly responsive girl she'd once been. Love was something that had to be arranged, prodded into shape; that was how she had come to love Michael—and that *was* love, she knew.

But so was this.

Will buried his head against Casey's neck, and when he spoke next, his voice was muffled and she didn't understand what he'd said, so she asked him to repeat it. He lifted his head. "Leave him" were the words.

"*What?*" she said.

"Leave him," said Will. "Come with me, Casey, back to San Francisco. There's a plane tomorrow morning."

"Tomorrow," said Casey slowly, "is my anniversary party. One hundred people will be coming to my backyard."

"Is that what you want?" said Will. "Is that what you want to celebrate?"

She pictured Michael's face, the concentration in

his eyes as he worked a lathe in his wood shop. Steady, worthy Michael, whom she loved in a way that had always been limited, because she kept it limited. She'd withheld herself from him—maybe, she thought now, because in the back of her mind she was waiting for Will. Because Will had once kissed her and worshiped her in a bed that no longer existed, but which she could still feel, the topography of the bad mattress, the sheet twisting between her legs and Will pulling it slowly through, laughing. What she and Will had had was about sex, and love, and being self-absorbed and young. Now they were no longer young, but what else did they have left? Casey and Michael's twenty-year marriage was courtly, affectionate, lacking a certain brand of heat that she'd almost, but not quite, forgotten. You got only one chance in life, Casey kept thinking now. How could she turn away from Will Combray, a man who had miraculously risen from the dead, or at least from San Francisco?

"Please, Casey," he was saying. "Leave with me in the morning. I have a beautiful house overlooking the bay and the Golden Gate Bridge. Wall-to-wall windows. We can sit there together and look out over the water and talk and talk. We can make up for all the time we've lost."

"But there's Michael . . ." she said weakly.

"He'll suffer," replied Will. "I know he will. And I'm sorry about that. But he won't die from it; he really won't."

"My children," said Casey. "Alex."

"You told me Alex is going off to college in two weeks," Will reminded her, and she thought again of how quiet the house would be after her son was gone. She'd been dreading his departure, not only because she would miss him but also because when he was gone and the house was empty and free of distractions, she knew she'd have to confront the truth of her marriage in a way she hadn't been willing to do: that there was, and always had been, something missing. It was a lack that not even a hundred people and a pile of presents could fill.

Casey loved Michael, had of course always loved him, but sometimes love alone wasn't enough. Love alone couldn't take a woman and lift her up from the shadows of an inexplicable melancholy. It was *her* lack, not his, that complicated their marriage; something was missing inside her that Michael could never complete, not because of who he was but because of who *she* was. Something was missing inside her that Will Combray, once, *had* completed. Will had worked his rather obvious charms, but those were charms she thought she'd long ago outgrown; she thought she'd been forced to outgrow them, but here they were again, on display, and Casey found that she didn't want to turn away.

She sat down then, wearily, leaning against the cracked wall where once a dresser had stood, and Will sat down beside her. They leaned together as though they were two very tired people who'd been traveling, and they held hands. The light in the room had shifted, Casey realized. She was tired and overwhelmed and waiting for some sort of wisdom to arrive and help her out of this mess she had gotten herself into. He'd asked her to leave Michael and go away with him, and the idea was strangely appealing. It would be an honest action on her part, though infinitely cruel; it would address the lack that had always been in her marriage but that she and Michael had never addressed. They were both too polite, too considerate, and they loved each other too much to have opened up the other person to such potential hurt. And now, as a result, she knew that if she left him she would be consigning him to more pain than any earlier discussion would have caused. Michael would stumble about the house, lost, betrayed, insisting to his friends and his children that he didn't understand why she had left, and yet, of course, he *would* understand, at least a little.

"Tell me about your life," said Casey now. "I want to know. I'll have to know—" She almost said,—*if you expect me to go away with you.*

Will exhaled heavily. He leaned his head back against the wall, studying the ceiling—the same ceiling, she thought, he would have studied endlessly the night he struggled with the decision of whether to marry her. And that was in fact where he began his story.

"Okay, fair enough," he said. "The night before our wedding, after I'd decided I couldn't handle it, I headed off on my bike, and days later I ended up in the Pacific Northwest, where I got a job hauling salmon. I did that for a while, feeling completely numb the whole time. I stank of fish; no one would get near me. I drank every night with all the fishermen. And one day I realized, Oh, I get it, this is just another version of being like my father. So the next day I left the fishing boat, without telling them I was going. Just the way I left you.

"And I went to San Francisco and walked right into a bank there at nine one morning and asked to see the manager. It was an act of total nerve, really, but this little guy in horn-rimmed glasses comes out, and I start telling him that I'd like to go into finance, and that I don't know one thing about it, but I know I'd be good because I'm intuitive, and would he please consider hiring me? So he did, at a very low-level job, and I *was* really good at what I did. And for the first time in my life, I wore a suit and tie every day. And I learned everything there was to learn about finance, really absorbing the information, and pretty soon I realized that I didn't have any time to think about writing the Great American Novel, or even the Great American Poem for that matter. And as the years passed, I become more and more successful at what I did. And that literary side of me started to fade away like a muscle that softens into fat if you don't keep exercising it. One day I woke up and I was this successful venture capitalist, a millionaire living in a modern house made of glass brick that overlooked the Golden Gate Bridge. The little bit of energy I had left, I devoted to my so-called personal life."

Will took a breath. "As I've already explained, sort of, my first wife, Cynthia, loved to party," he went on. "She thought we were going to have a great time together, living in our swanky house and traveling around the world. What she didn't count on was the fact that I would have very little time for her. She did whatever she could to get my attention, but it just didn't work. One day I was sitting in my office when a process server showed up and told me I was being sued for divorce." He shook his head slowly. "I deserved it," he said. "My second wife, Julie, was more grounded. Which is why I thought things would be okay. But somehow they weren't. She said I didn't make her happy, that I didn't 'let her inside,' let her know my thoughts. She said that when she was with me she was lonely. That it just wasn't working." He sighed deeply. "The marriage was a failure. Like so much of my life."

"That's not true," said Casey.

"It is true," Will said. "And all the while I thought about you. And then one day I got the bright idea to

look you up on the Internet—but no dice. You'd
changed your name. So I contacted the high school
here, and that's how I found your address. I was
kind of surprised when I did find out what your last
name was."

"Yes, I can imagine," Casey said.

"And I was also surprised that you were living in
the same house you grew up in. Did your parents
move to a retirement home or something?"

So he didn't know. Of course he didn't; why
would he? It wasn't as though Eleanor and Warren
Stowe's deaths had made any newspapers other
than the *Longwood Falls Ledger.*

"No," she said softly, looking down at her hands,
for even now she could hardly speak about it. "They
were killed in a car accident."

Will looked at her sharply. "My God, Casey, I'm
so sorry. When was this? Recently?"

She shook her head, felt her eyes start to brim
over. "A lifetime ago," she said. "That winter after
you left me."

"I had no idea," said Will, his voice barely a whisper. "When I saw where you lived now, I just assumed you'd bought the house from them—that

they'd moved to, I don't know, Florida or something. My God," he went on, "I can't even imagine
what you've been through."

"No," she said softly. "You can't."

He sighed, deeply. And then he said, "But you
could tell me. Not today, not just today, but for as
long as it takes. We could spend so much time talking." He turned to her. "Come with me."

He held her hand more tightly, the afternoon getting old, and she had no idea of what to do, how to
move beyond this moment. She was supposed to be
in Cedar Vale, picking up her pale blue party dress.
In a few hours, Michael would come home from
work, his car pulling up the gravel driveway, sending a few pebbles pinging against the hubcaps, and
then she would hear his car door close and his footsteps coming up the walk, and then he would be inside the house, calling her name. It would be like
every other day of their marriage, and every day
that was to follow. And all of a sudden, she couldn't
bear that idea.

"All right," she finally said to Will in a voice she
scarcely recognized. "I'll come with you."

He looked at her, astonished. His face appeared

ecstatic, young, and the muscles of his jaw relaxed in the manner of someone who can't believe his good luck. He'd gotten her back, he really had. He'd come all this way, across the country and across time, and tomorrow morning—because she, too, wanted to know the answer to the question "What if?"—she was going to shock everyone she knew and go away with him. Will kissed her hand in response, held it to his mouth for a moment.

"Am I a bad person?" she asked him in a whisper. "Doing this to Michael? Oh, don't answer that."

Will shook his head no. "You're the only truly good person I've ever known," he said.

Casey sat with him in the deepening light of the empty room, imagining another room, one in San Francisco. She saw herself sitting with him in front of that window, watching the lights of the bridge in the distance and telling herself she was finally home, and almost starting to believe it.

Chapter
Eight

෴ To Casey's relief, Michael wasn't at the house yet when she got there, but the tent men were, taking metal poles and furled green-and-white-striped canvas off a truck and carrying it all around to the backyard.

"It'll be a good day for a party," one of the men called to her. "Weather's supposed to be perfect tomorrow."

She knew she ought to send them away right now, to announce that the party was off, but she wasn't brave enough to do that yet. She had come home without her dress, without the flowers, without the extra case of champagne she was supposed to pick up at the liquor store. And now, empty-handed, she smiled with the rote warmth of a flight attendant welcoming passengers aboard, and she followed the men around back. It was while she stood in the yard, dazed and jittery and over-whelmed, looking at the decorations that would have to be taken down—the streamers that hung from trees, and the silver-and-gold HAPPY ANNIVER-SARY sign that Alex and his girlfriend Amy had made—that she saw her father-in-law, Tom Becket, at the fountain. He was bending over the edge of the stone basin and peering inside, holding some small, arcane tools that she didn't recognize. Since his re-tirement last year, it was clear that Tom needed to feel needed, and repairing the fountain in time for the party was something he'd been looking forward to. It wasn't a big job, really, and he had told Casey and Michael that he would be able to accomplish it in one day. Today was that day.

For a moment, Casey thought about quickly ducking inside the house and avoiding her father-in-law altogether. She was reminded of a similar mo-ment so many years earlier, when she was heading off to meet Will for their first dinner together and she saw Tom and Janice Becket sitting on the front porch of their house and she'd managed to get away with simply wishing them a good evening. Now here she was, more than twenty years later, still preparing to sneak off to see Will. It was almost as if nothing had changed in all that time. But, of course, everything had changed. However guilty and fearful she might have felt on the night she went to meet Will at The Granary, it was nothing compared to what she was feeling now, because now she had so much more to lose. But she also knew that it would take a great deal more than a simple mention of Michael's name to make her change her mind.

"Just give me another hour or so," Tom called to Casey when he saw her approach. "Cleaned out all the leaves, scrubbed the whole thing a bit, and now I'm concentrating on the waterworks, which are fairly jammed up. Nothing fatal, though. It's really fallen into disrepair, hasn't it?" he added.

"Sorry," Casey said quietly. "We didn't mean to. It just happened."

Tom Becket looked at her, aware that her voice sounded peculiar. "I wasn't blaming you and

Michael," he said softly. "Janice and I have equal custody of this fountain. It means a lot to us, too, you know. Hell, I built it."

"No, of course," she said. What Casey really wanted to say to Tom now was *Leave it. There's not going to be any party.* Why was he babbling on about the fountain, which she didn't care about at all and hadn't in fact cared about for a long time? When she saw the fountain, she thought only of the loss associated with it: the loss of Michael as her friend, and then of Will, who was supposed to have married her there, and then, finally, of her parents. There were times she hated the fountain, when she didn't care if she ever saw it again. Maybe, Casey thought now, she never *would* see it again. But here was Tom Becket, oblivious to everything that she was thinking, steadfastly working on the basin of the fountain with his tools, as conscientious as his son. Both of these men, when they said they were going to do something, they did it. Tom said the fountain would be fixed today, so here he was; Michael had said he would always take care of Casey, and so he had. Often, over the years, Casey had wished she could be more like them, always throwing themselves into the physical labor of a project, attacking problems with a whistling certainty that they could fix anything, given enough tools and time. They were loyal and skillful and admirable, while she—she was not.

"Where'd you go?" asked her father-in-law.

"San Francisco," Casey said, before she had a chance to realize what she was saying.

"What's that?" he said.

Casey felt her face grow hot, and she was suddenly overcome with vertigo. "I think I need to sit down," she said, and her father-in-law quickly unfolded a white folding chair—one of a hundred that had been rented for the occasion—and helped her into it.

"What's the matter, Casey?" he asked her. "Are you sick?"

Casey put her face in her hands and let herself cry silently for a moment or two while Tom stared at her, shocked. Certainly it hadn't been her intention to tell anyone before she'd had a chance to tell Michael, but here Tom was, watching her with obvious alarm, and here she was, openly crying and unable to remain on her feet, and all of a sudden there seemed to be no other way.

%

"Tom," she said. "Oh, Tom. I have to tell you something."

"Oh," he said, and he put down his tools and shakily unfolded his own chair, sitting down across from her.

"I'm leaving here tomorrow morning," she began slowly.

"What?" he said. "What do you mean? Where are you going? The party's tomorrow."

"There's not going to be any party," Casey said. "I'm leaving Michael."

Tom looked as though she'd told him that someone he loved had died; he looked, she realized, the way she herself must have looked when the state troopers came to her door on that winter night so many years ago.

"When he comes home this evening," she continued in a quieter voice, "I'm going to tell him. I wasn't planning on telling you now, but under the circumstances, I didn't know what else to do."

"But why?" asked her father-in-law, and his voice was as thin and reedy as the voice of a much older man. Maybe it was the voice he was meant to have, for she often forgot he was a senior citizen, remem-

224

bering instead the young, robust father next door from her childhood, standing proudly at his backyard grill in a pair of Bermuda shorts.

"Because of Will Combray," said Casey, realizing how odd this sounded. She wasn't even sure Tom would remember who that was. It had been far too long ago, and most likely Michael, still feeling vestiges of the pain of the entire episode, had never mentioned Will to his parents again.

But Tom did remember. "I see," he said, nodding slowly. "That fellow from when you were young. The one who left you stranded at the altar, so to speak. What, you've been sending e-mail to each other, is that it? You've renewed your acquaintance, you've started thinking about old times?"

"He's come back," said Casey. "After all these years. Yesterday he showed up right here in this yard. Tom, I thought I would faint when I looked out the kitchen window and saw him there. I haven't seen him since the day he didn't marry me. And there he was, as though he'd been brought back by some kind of magic. And we started talking and telling each other about our lives, and today we talked some more, and I know how terrible it is of me to say this to you of all people, but I just can't help myself: He asked me to go away with him, to live with him in San Francisco, and against my best judgment I've decided that I want to."

"But why?" Tom asked, then held up a hand. "No, no, don't answer that, Casey. It's an impertinent question. You know I've always tried to stay out of your business. Janice and I wanted to let you and Michael have your own lives and not interfere, especially since you live next door and the temptation to meddle is so high. And that's not going to change. It isn't my place to ask you why. I suppose I was speaking out of a father's concern for his boy." He glanced up at the fountain and the statue there of baby Michael as an angel. *Michael still looks like that,* Casey thought as she regarded the angel; *he still has the same smooth forehead and uncorrupted face.*

"I guess that seems strange," Tom went on. "Michael's hardly a boy; he's a grown man, a father of someone who's almost a grown man, too. But when he was first born, I used to tuck him inside my peacoat and go for a stroll down Main Street with his little bald head poking out the collar. I liked being able to keep him safe like that, and warm. But I can't do that now. It isn't my role."

"No, it's my role," said Casey. "And I'm giving it up. It's the last thing in the world I ever imagined I'd want to do, Tom, please believe me."

But again he interrupted her. "I don't have to believe you, Casey," he said, his voice sounding both irritated and weary. "It doesn't matter what I believe. You know your heart, and you know what you need. My boy will suffer. I can't put him inside my coat. No one can. But that's not what this is about, taking care of Michael, is it?" She shook her head. "I just want to ask you one thing, though," he said, "and then I should be getting back home. I'm suddenly tired, and it's getting late in the day." He paused. "Are you sure you're doing the right thing, going off with this Will character?"

"No," she said simply. "I'm not sure. Michael is the kindest man in the world; he gets that from you. But Will isn't evil or anything; he's complicated, like anyone is. Look, if anyone has a right to be furious with Will, it's me. And I have been. I've carried that anger around with me, more than I think I even realized. But he explained everything to me, told me what happened all those years ago, and why he left."

"He told you that?" said Tom with surprise, and Casey nodded. "And just what did he say?"

"Well," said Casey, "he told me he was scared to get married. Scared to face the responsibility. He said that he wasn't ready for a stable life."

"And how did he come to this realization?" Tom asked.

"Lying in his room in the boardinghouse the night before the wedding," she said. "He stayed there all night and thought and thought. And he felt that he wasn't up to the task. He was too frightened of it. He felt he was weak and not good enough for me. And so he decided to leave."

"Ah." Tom nodded a few times, almost to himself. Then he stood slowly, folding the chair after he was standing and returning it to its pile. "Well, as I said, I should be going." His face was stony, unfamiliar, almost impassive. She wanted to ask him to forgive her, to tell him that she loved him, that he'd been a wonderful father-in-law and she would miss him dearly, but she did none of those things. Instead, she watched him walk back over to the fountain, gather his tools into a toolbox, and then head back across the lawn into his own house, the screen door slowly shuddering shut.

For a moment, Casey didn't budge. She stayed sitting on her folding chair on the lawn, while in the distance the men banged the poles into the ground and raised a tent to block out the sky in case it rained tomorrow or was blisteringly hot. But it didn't matter what the weather would be; the tent would have to come down.

She leaned back in her chair and closed her eyes, as if she could shut out the activity in the yard. Her talk with Tom hadn't gone at all the way she would have liked; but at least it had *gone*. It was over, somehow, and for that she was grateful and relieved. She saw now that it was possible to have this conversation and not fall apart. She would have to have it again, with all three of her children, and of course somehow with Michael, and she supposed that if she thought too much about their life together in this house on the street where they'd both grown up, she might well fall apart. How could she do this to them? she asked herself. How could she hurt the people she loved so much?

But then she reminded herself that her children were pretty much adults now themselves. She'd watched the girls do what all children sooner or later do—and what Alex was about to do—which was leave. First you teach them to latch on, Casey reflected now; then you teach them to let go. And so she had, and so they had, and now they were on their own, Hannah and Rachel picking subjects to major in, and Alex falling in love with Amy and occasionally prying himself away from her for a few minutes so he could pack for college. And while the thought of their mother suddenly and cruelly leaving their father would disturb them, and even enrage them, and perhaps turn one or any of them against her, she knew that at least the conversation she'd have with them would, like the one she'd just had with Tom, pass.

Not so the one with Michael. That one, there was no telling how it would go. The news would wound him severely—and there was simply no escaping that—and for that she was already remorseful. He would have every right to ask himself, Is there no time when a person can let his guard down? When he can trust the other person absolutely? When he can tell himself that she is his now, and nothing can change that?

No.

That was the simple answer, Casey thought. No, there is no such time. Michael had learned that once already with Casey, and she herself had learned it with Will. And now here they all were, this same cast of characters, learning it all over again. What if, she thought, by some stroke of fate, Casey *had* married Will on that long-ago Saturday afternoon? What if he had shown up in this yard as he was supposed to, and the minister had spoken, and Eleanor Stowe and Janice Becket had cried?

Here's what: Even without Casey, Michael would have remained alive and vibrant, even though he would have sworn at the time that he wouldn't. Eventually, no doubt, he would have found another woman and started a life with her, and that life might have turned out just as rewarding as the one he and Casey had made for themselves. Rachel, Hannah, and Alex, as unthinkable as it was to her, wouldn't exist, but other children of Michael's would, and nobody would be any the wiser. Who could say which version of the universe would have been preferable? Nobody knew; nobody could ever know.

Somewhere, two tent poles clanged together, making a sound like a bell. A shadow fell across her face, and Casey opened her eyes. Tom Becket was standing before her.

"Can we go inside?" her father-in-law said to her. "We need to talk."

Chapter
Nine

❧

ᔐ Tom Becket held open the screen door, and Casey nodded and stepped into the kitchen. Her father-in-law was just being the polite person that he was, but something about the formality of the gesture chilled her, made her feel as if she were a guest in her own home.

And it *was* her home. It might not be for much longer, but for now it still was. It was the house she'd lived in from the time she was born, and she knew its corners, the creaks of its floors, and the hissing of steam in its pipes at night, as well as she knew anything. She had been carried on her father's shoulders through these rooms and had watched Michael carry the children on his shoulders, too. Was it really possible that she was willing to walk away from it all?

Yes, Casey told herself. Yes, it was. Just because she happened to be standing in her kitchen with Tom Becket didn't make all the reasons for leaving that she'd felt so strongly when she was sitting on the floor at the boardinghouse any less real.

Suddenly, Casey wanted nothing more than to be alone. She wanted the clanging of the tent poles to stop and the workers from the catering company off her property. She didn't want Tom Becket making himself at home in her kitchen, settling in at the big maple table as he had done so many times before, and she certainly didn't want to hear what he had to say, not now, perhaps not ever. He was right: It was none of his business what she did with her life or how her actions might affect his son, and she regretted having been indiscreet and revealing her secret to him before Michael knew.

"Would you like some iced tea?" she said stiffly, opening the refrigerator door and starting to pull out the big glass pitcher of raspberry tea, lemon slices floating on the surface like lily pads.

"No, thank you," Tom said, matching her tone. Then he said, "Sit down, Casey."

She slid the pitcher back and let the refrigerator door sigh shut. Then she joined him at the kitchen table, taking the chair directly opposite his, and waited.

"Now," Tom began. He placed his hands flat down on the surface and absently rubbed the maple wood, as if he were sanding this piece of furniture. He has his son's hands, Casey thought, then corrected herself: Michael has his father's hands. "Now," Tom said again, as if he were having trouble getting started. He waited another moment, then somehow found it inside himself to forge ahead. "I'm about to break an old promise," he told her. "I'm going to do something I swore to Michael I'd never do, and which I never had the slightest intention of doing." He glanced up at Casey, then down at his hands again. "I'm going to tell you what happened on the night before you were supposed to marry Will Combray."

Casey felt herself straighten in her chair. "I know what happened," she said evenly. "As I said, Will already told me."

But even as these words were leaving her, she heard how empty they sounded, as hollow as the tent poles ringing in the yard.

"Well, as I said," Tom went on, ignoring her protest, "it was the night before the wedding. I won't pretend it was a particularly happy time around our house. Michael wasn't himself, really, and hadn't been since the day he found out you were marrying someone else.

"Not that I thought Michael *should* marry you," Tom hurried on. "Unlike Janice and your mother, I for one didn't think you and Michael were necessarily made for each other. Just because you were best friends as children, and even as teenagers, didn't mean to me that you would make each other content as husband and wife. Though I guess you did, finally. Or at least I always thought you seemed to."

"We did," Casey felt compelled to reply, because it was true, in many ways.

Tom nodded once, accepting her answer. "Be that as it may," he said, "I never thought you and

ᢌ

Michael were automatically made for each other in some till-death-do-us-part kind of way just because you were the same age and next-door neighbors, and when you chose instead to marry this other fellow, this stranger from up near Canada with the pollution-spewing motorcycle and the superior attitude . . . well, I regretted the hurt it was causing my son, but I also thought that, you know, it might be best for him in the long run."

The long run. Like father, like son, Casey thought.

"I mean," Tom went on, "if you didn't want to spend your life with him, then you were not the girl for him, period, and no amount of wailing and tearing his hair out was going to make it so. Because you can't change people."

"No, you can't," Casey agreed, wondering where all of this was going.

Tom took in a breath, then let it out slowly. "So," he said. "It was the night before your wedding. As I said, it wasn't a happy time around our house. Me, I didn't much like your husband-to-be, from what I saw of him, and I think I can safely say the same was true for Janice. But it's what the wedding was doing to Michael that had us troubled most of all. We didn't want to see him suffer, even if we knew that what was happening was somehow for the best. So we tried to do things to make it easier for him. He'd had a difficult time at college during the year, what with coping with your news, and he'd had a bad time up at Indian Lake in the summer, trying to stay focused on the kids he was taking care of, but all the time thinking of . . . well, you know."

He shook his head, as if the memory were still fresh. And it was, she supposed. After all, it was still fresh to her.

"So what I did that night," Tom continued, "is ask him to go out with me on an emergency plumbing run that had just been phoned in. I didn't need to. I mean, it wasn't that big a deal. But I thought it might do Michael some good. Get him out of the house. So I stopped by his room, where he'd been sitting on his bed for half the day with the same magazine open on his lap. Didn't even come down for dinner. Instead, he just sat there and said, 'I'm not hungry,' and you know how good a cook Janice is. She'd made his favorite that night, shrimp scampi. But the shrimp were just curled up on the plate, like Michael in his room. Until finally Janice picked the plate up and took it back into the kitchen, slamming it down on the counter. Now, you know she isn't a woman who's prone to cursing, but she let loose a string of curse words that night, the only time I ever remember her doing so."

Tom paused. "She was looking out the window and into the backyard," he went on, "and just like today it had a tent pitched, and it was full of workers getting ready for the big celebration the next day. And I knew she was thinking about how we'd all made this place together, she and I and your parents—this yard that the two families shared over the years— and that now it had this. . . ." He paused, searching for the word. "*Taint*," he said, curling his upper lip. "This taint on it. And I knew she was thinking about how we'd never be able to look out our window without thinking of what we'd once had out there, and how it was all ruined. And Janice was looking out at the yard, and then she suddenly started saying things—things about you—that made me raise my eyebrows."

Michael's father returned his gaze from the

counter to Casey. Casey met his gaze. He went on talking.

"I told her, 'It's not Casey's fault. It's not anybody's fault. It just is.'

"But Janice shook her head and said, 'Can't you stop being so goddamn reasonable for just one minute of your life, Tom?'

"Well, I didn't know what to say to that. Except, maybe, 'Touché.' Because I *was* trying to be reasonable about it—'My son's learning a hard lesson' and all that, treating him as if he were some kind of busted faucet or something, as if, with the right twist of a screwdriver, he'd be good as new—and that's not what Michael needed. He needed *me*. He needed to be with me that night, to 'hang out' with, as you kids used to say. And suddenly, I saw that. And so I went upstairs to ask him to go out with me on the emergency job.

"So we went," said Tom. "We got in the truck and we headed a few blocks away to fix some lady's stopped-up bathtub. Along the way, he and I didn't talk much. I figured if he wanted to say something, he would, and that it wasn't up to me to force him. It was good enough, I decided, that I'd gotten him out and about. Mission accomplished. The rest would be a breeze. We'd go in, fix the bathtub, get out. Maybe stop off somewhere for a hamburger and a Coke on the way back, just to kill time. Well," Tom added, "it didn't quite work out that way."

He made a short laughing sound now, but he wasn't smiling. "When we got to the house," Tom said, "I went ahead and rang the doorbell, while Michael went and got the tools out of the back of the truck. The door opened, and a young woman stood there. She looked familiar to me, but I didn't know from where, and I said some lame thing to her, like 'I hear you have a sick bathtub,' and she said, 'I'm glad you make house calls.' She was a friendly woman, very pretty, and I would have asked where the bathroom was and gotten right to work but for the fact that suddenly she was looking past me as though she'd seen a ghost. And I turned around to see what she was looking at. And it was Michael."

"Michael?" Casey found herself repeating.

"He was standing in the doorway with the tools," said Tom, "and he was looking at her like he recognized her from somewhere, and he was saying, 'Hello, Miss Bradley, remember me? I'm Michael Becket. We've met through Casey Stowe.'"

"*Dorian* Bradley, my piano teacher?" said Casey with surprise.

"That's right, your piano teacher," Tom Becket said. He stopped here and lifted a hand to his face. He rubbed the side of his cheek, like someone debating whether or not to shave. After a few moments, he folded both hands together and looked directly at Casey.

"I think I'll take that glass of iced tea now," he said.

Dorian Bradley, with her henna-colored hair and her stories of life out in the real world: Once, a long time ago, Casey had gotten a note from her, saying she was finally getting out of Longwood Falls. Over the years, Casey had often wished that she'd gotten to know her better. Now, for better or worse, Casey suspected she would have the chance.

She brought the pitcher to the table along with two tall glasses. She poured one glass for Tom, then one for herself. Tom raised his to his forehead, closed his eyes, and ran the glass along his skin from one temple to the other. Then he brought the rim of the glass to his mouth and took a long series of swallows. Casey watched his Adam's apple go to work, and she thought: Plumbing. That's all we are. We thirst; we sweat; we swallow. And as long as the plumbing works, we work; and when it doesn't, we don't.

"Thank you, that's just what I needed," he said, putting his iced tea back on the table. He'd drunk more than half the glass. He closed his eyes, and when he resumed speaking, he kept them closed.

"I can still see it like it just happened," he said. "Dorian Bradley is standing there looking at Michael in this strange way, and in my ignorance I think it's because she feels sorry for him—that must be it. She knows that Casey's marrying someone else tomorrow, and she doesn't know how to react in front of this poor, lovesick boy."

Tom shook his head. "But that's not it," he went on. "Not at all. Because all of a sudden there's the sound of footsteps coming down the stairs, and I look up and who do I see?"

"Who?" Casey said, though she wasn't sure she really wanted to know.

"Will Combray," said her father-in-law.

"Will knew my piano teacher?" Casey heard herself say feebly.

Tom didn't answer. Eyes still closed, he continued his story. "And all he's wearing is a pair of boxer shorts. And when he gets to the bottom of the stairs, he looks at us—me for a second, then Michael—and my mind starts spinning because there's no mistaking it now: We've got a situation on our hands here. A bad one. Here's Will Combray, the guy who's marrying Casey Stowe tomorrow morning, wearing only his shorts and no shirt and casually walking around the house of a woman who's not Casey Stowe—a woman who in fact is a good ten years older than he is.

"And Michael just stares at him. And finally, Will says, 'It's not what you think, Becket.'

"And Michael says, 'I don't think anything, *Combray*.' They suddenly have to be macho or something, calling each other by their last names. 'It's none of my business,' Michael says. And then he turns around and starts to leave the house.

"But Will says it again. 'It's not what you think.'

"Now, this makes Michael turn around and say, 'What do you mean?'

"And Will says, 'Well, it *is* what you think, I guess. Dorian is an old friend of mine, nothing more than that. But it's the night before my wedding, and you know how it is.'

"'No, I'm afraid I wouldn't know that,' says Michael.

"But Will ignores him. Says, 'And I was all alone and feeling the jitters, so I called Dorian to see if I could just come over and maybe watch a little TV with her, and she said yes. And I came over and we were just sitting around, and I don't know, it never happened before, and maybe it was just because I was nervous and keyed up and all, but suddenly something started happening, and then one thing led to another, and, and, and—and then you showed up.'

"And Michael looks at him.

"And Will says, 'And as I said, it's never happened before, and it will never happen again. You've got to believe me.'

"But while he's saying this, he's not looking at

Michael. He's looking at Dorian. And I guess that's when I should have known."

"Known what?" said Casey.

But Tom didn't answer her. Maybe he didn't hear her. He was sitting perfectly still, his eyes still closed, lost in the scene from more than twenty years earlier.

"And Michael tells Will," Tom continued, " 'I don't care. This is between you and Casey. Or not. It's your business.' And he starts to leave again, but Will reaches out and stops him.

" 'So you won't tell Casey?' he says.

"And Michael—he takes a deep breath, and he keeps staring at the floor, and you can see he's doing everything he can to rise to the occasion, but he wants out, really bad—and Michael says, 'No. I won't tell Casey.'

" 'Word of honor?'

"And now Michael looks up at Will. He can't believe what he's hearing. 'Honor,' from this guy, who's spending the night before his wedding in bed with another woman. But he can see it's important to Will, and it's none of his business, anyway, after all. So Michael just says, real slow and clear, looking Will right in the eye, 'Word of honor.' "

The Fountain

~

"And he goes outside. I start to follow him, mumbling something to Dorian Bradley, telling her we'll send another plumber, and I hurry out onto the front path after Michael. He's standing there with his head in his hands, really having a rough time, I can see, and his shoulders are shaking. And I tell him we should get out of here, we should go somewhere and talk, but as I'm saying this, we start to hear voices coming out of the house.

"Dorian Bradley is shouting at Will, saying something like 'Go! Get out of here and leave me alone! Just go!' And he's saying, 'Not until we talk about this.' And she says, 'There's nothing to talk about.' And he says, 'Nothing to talk about, when it's obvious that we still love each other?'

"And here we are, still right out in front of the house, hearing every word. Maybe not fully understanding what they're saying, but it doesn't matter. Me, I'm just trying to get Michael back in the truck. 'Come on, son,' I'm saying. 'Come on. Come on.'

"But it's too late. Before I know what's happening, Michael is off like a shot. Back into the house. And as he goes through the front door? That's when I see it in his hand."

Tom opened his eyes now. Casey looked at him, hard.

"He's got a wrench," Tom said.

And now it was Casey who had to close her eyes.

"I take off after him. But he's a young man, and he's got a head start on me. By the time I get into the living room, I can already hear the screams. He's all over Will, hitting him with it, and I grab Michael, grab his arm, pull it back. And I'm hearing screams all around me now, and then someone else is there, grabbing at Michael, and I see that it's Dorian, but Michael's too strong. And finally, I hear a new voice, yelling, screaming. And it takes me a second to realize it's me, and what I'm saying is 'Michael! Look at yourself! Look what you're doing!'

"And that seems to do something. To get through. He weakens a little, and Dorian and I pull him back, hold his arm down, and he falls back against the couch, and then he's sitting there, breathing heavy. And I hold out my hand. And he looks at my hand, and then down at the wrench in his hand like it's the first time he's seen it, like maybe he doesn't even know how it got there. And he gives it to me. And then we're all looking at it, because it's shining with blood. Will's blood.

"We all look at Will. He's still on the floor, leaning against a chair, and his chin is bleeding. Dorian lets go a little 'Oh.' You know? And she runs and gets him a washrag and some ice, and he holds it there for a while. Then, finally, when he can speak, he says to Michael, 'I guess I deserved that.'

" 'I guess you did,' Michael says.

" 'But now, maybe,' Will goes on, 'you want to hear the real story.'

" 'It doesn't matter what the real story is,' Michael tells him, but you can see in Michael's eyes—and Will says it then—that yes, it does matter. Will says, 'I want you to know the truth,' and he looks at Dorian. And she turns away, but she doesn't leave the room. So Will just sits there, breathing heavy, holding the ice against his chin. And then he begins talking, and what he says is this:

" 'Okay. I admit it. Dorian and I used to be lovers. And it was pretty intense. We met a couple of years ago when I was riding through town—months before I ever met Casey. For a while there things were okay, but then we started arguing. She was afraid that I was too young for her, that people would talk. She said wasn't it funny, here she was someone who liked to think of herself as an original, a bohemian, but when push came to shove it was hard for her to do something that might be described as scandalous. Not to mention the fact that she was afraid I'd grow tired of her, that I'd want someone younger. Things went on like that with us for a while. One day, I came to her house to see her, and we argued again, so I went downtown to cool off. And that was when I met Casey. I had no idea she was Dorian's student; how could I possibly have known? But there I was, just walking along and thinking about how Dorian and I could never really be together, that we'd always be arguing, always on the verge of splitting up, and then—there was Casey. And I don't know, we just started talking, and the more we talked, the more I thought, Yes, this is what it's supposed to be like. Love, I mean.'"

Tom stopped for a moment, looking at Casey as though he hoped to gauge her reaction so far.

"I'm afraid the story gets a little more unpleasant, Casey," Tom said.

The Fountain

ॐ

Casey couldn't move, couldn't even blink. All she wanted was for him to go on. Whatever he had to tell her, it had to be said. She nodded, and Tom continued speaking.

"So. So then Will says to Michael, 'I wanted out. Dorian didn't. I told her about Casey, and she begged me to change my mind. She said she didn't want to lose me. And I guess maybe I came back here tonight because in some way I didn't want to lose her, either.'

"'Didn't?' Michael says. 'Or *don't*?'

"And Will doesn't answer at first. Just sits there, holding the washrag against his chin. He looks up at Dorian, who's still got her back turned toward him. Just looks at her for a long time. And then he says, '*Don't*. Don't want to lose her.'"

Tom stopped talking again. And again he looked at Casey as though for some sort of response. But she had none, really; how could she? Tom's story seemed surreal, made her feel as though she were drowning. She just shook her head slowly, then said, "Tom, I can't imagine what I can possibly say."

"No," said her father-in-law. "I suppose you can't." He paused for a moment, then went on.

Emily Grayson

*

"Well, the two of them just sit there in Dorian's living room for a while," he said, "Michael and Will, neither of them saying anything. But finally, it's Michael who breaks the silence. He says to Will, 'What are we going to do?'

"'Do?' Will asks.

"'Yes,' says Michael. 'You think it wouldn't hurt Casey to know you're here? To know that you're still in love with Dorian? Still obsessed with her? That you want to find a way to keep seeing her, even after the wedding tomorrow?'

"And I hear a little cry coming from Dorian, and Will looks at her and then looks back at Michael, and he says, 'Yes. Of course, it would hurt her to know that. And if you think I don't feel really bad about it, you're wrong. But who's going to be the one to tell her? You?'

"And Michael sits there running his hand through his hair, trying to get his thoughts together, and then finally he says, 'I just don't want to see Casey get hurt.'

"Will says, 'Neither do I.'

"'So what are we going to do about this?' Michael asks.

254

The Fountain

" 'There's nothing for *us* to do,' says Will. 'It's not really your business.'

" 'No,' Michael says. 'You're wrong. Casey may be your wife by this time tomorrow, but she's still my closest friend, my oldest friend in the world. I swear to God, I won't let you hurt her. And you know as well as I do, both of you'—and here he's looking at Dorian now, too—'you know that if this doesn't stop, then Casey will definitely get badly hurt. It's only a matter of time. You do know this, right? It won't be from me, but you do know that one day she's going to find out, and when she does, it will destroy her. Destroy her.'

" 'Yes.' It's Dorian talking now. She turns around and says it again. 'Yes, I do know that. And I won't let it happen. So this thing, this relationship, is over. As of right now. What Will and I have—*had*—is done.'

"And Will says, 'Dorian.'

"And she says, 'I'm sorry, Will. But I'm not sorry, too. The time has come. And you know I'm right.'

"Will doesn't say anything at first. And then he does. He says, 'Yes. You're right.'

"And both of them look like they're about to cry,

but they hold back. And after a second, Michael pushes himself up off the couch, and then Will gets to his feet, too, and then he does the most amazing thing. Will holds out his hand.

" 'Word of honor,' Will says.

"And then Michael does the most amazing thing, too," Tom said with a disbelief that was still tangible all these decades later. "He—he takes Will's hand. And the two of them shake, right there, reaching out to each other in Dorian Bradley's living room.

"And with that, Michael walks out of the room and out of that house.

"In the truck, on the ride home, the only thing Michael says is, 'Will and me? Neither one of us deserves Casey Stowe.' "

Tom Becket took a long drink of the iced tea, draining the glass. When he was done, he stood up from the table, walked over to the kitchen door, and opened it. Then he stood there for a moment and turned back to Casey, who hadn't moved from the table and who wondered how she would ever be able to.

"I made two promises that night," Tom said now.

"The first was when I was leaving the house, heading back down the walk to the truck. Dorian caught up with me. 'I just want you to know,' she said, 'I've always felt guilty about keeping my history with Will a secret from Casey. But I never wanted to hurt Casey. Never. Promise me, please, promise me if Casey ever does find out about what happened here tonight, you'll tell her that. That I never wanted to hurt her. And that I love her.'"

"Thank you, Tom," Casey said now, softly.

He nodded but didn't look at her. He was standing by the back door, staring into the yard.

"And promise number two," he said. "I swore to Michael I would never tell you what happened that night." He turned to Casey. "And I never have, until now. I don't think it was just that Michael wanted to spare you the details of Will's life, though that was part of it. I think Michael was ashamed of *himself*. Of how he behaved, and what he almost did, swinging that wrench. Of the side of himself he saw that night. A violence he didn't know he possessed.

"And now I've broken my promise. I've told you all this not because I think what you do is any of my business, because it's not. And I haven't done this to help Michael. With the single exception of that night at Dorian Bradley's, I think my son has been able to take care of himself. And I haven't done this for your kids, because they're pretty much grown and they can handle themselves. And God knows I haven't done it for *this*"—and with a wave of his hand, Tom seemed to take in the kitchen and the yard and everything else on Strawberry Street—"because I just don't care anymore. Oh, I care, I guess. I care enough to come over and fix the fountain, if that's what you want. But I care only as much as anyone else cares. Beyond that, I don't. I really don't. Your parents are gone, and I'm retired. I remember when the four of us—your parents, Janice, me—would sit in the backyard and watch you and Michael chase each other around and around, playing hide-and-seek behind the hedge. We still had the hedge then. And how we'd sit there and watch you two and talk about how we wanted to leave you a better world than the one we grew up in. That's all. That's all we ever really wanted in the long run." He shrugged and turned away from her, back toward the yard. "My work is done, for better or worse, and nothing I can possibly say here today and nothing you can possibly say or do can change any of that. No," he went on, "I've done this for you, Casey. Not so you'll change your decision about leaving Michael for Will Combray, because that's your business. But just so you'll know. Just so you have all the information."

Tom thought for a moment, and then he apparently decided he was finished. He let himself out the back door, and it shut silently behind him. Casey, however, didn't move. She continued sitting at the kitchen table, just running her hand along its smooth surface. After all, she'd finally gotten exactly what she wished for earlier in the afternoon, when Tom had first set foot in the kitchen: the solitude of her own house. Even the banging of the tent poles, she noticed after a minute or two, had at some point stopped.

She was, indeed, all alone now.

Chapter
Ten

⮑ As the tent man had predicted, Saturday was a perfect day for a party, the sun bright white and the humidity nearly nonexistent. Around the back of the house on Strawberry Street, the people from the party rental company were putting the final touches on the arrangement of tables, chairs, and decorations. The backyard looked gorgeous, the green-and-white-striped tent rippling slightly in the breeze.

The only problem was that Casey Becket was nowhere to be found.

It was Alex who was the first to wonder where his

mother was. He was standing in the kitchen getting himself some orange juice and trying to stay out of the way of the caterers, who had commandeered the room. At one point, a young woman in a uniform that looked like a tuxedo asked him if there were any extra pot holders around, and Alex said he'd have to ask his mother. But where *was* his mother? He realized that he had no idea; he hadn't, in fact, seen her since late last night, when she had gone with him and his father to pick up Hannah and Rachel at the bus station downtown. But she'd seemed a little weird to him then, distracted and quiet. She'd claimed she was just tired, that all these weeks of preparing for the party had worn her down. And then, after the twins' bus arrived and everyone came back home, Casey spent hardly any time with her family. Usually, she couldn't get enough of Hannah or Rachel if one of them came home for a visit, and here she had both of them at once, yet after only a few minutes, she said she had to go to bed. As far as Alex knew, that's where she still was, though it wasn't like her to sleep in on such an important day.

Upstairs, alone in the bedroom, Michael Becket

was getting ready, dawdling before the mirror and experimenting with different ways to knot his tie. The truth was that he didn't want this day to rush past too quickly; he wanted to savor it like a fine meal, to slow it down, to make it last a long time and have it become something he would remember forever. Casey was already up, had apparently awakened before him, and was probably down-stairs right now dealing with the caterers. Maybe their marriage at times had not been the most romantic in the world, he knew, but their anniversary party would be.

As Michael lingered over the knotting of his tie before the mirror, there was a knock on the door. "Come in," he said.

Alex appeared in the doorway. "Hi, Dad," he said, poking his head into the room. "Where's Mom?"

"Oh, downstairs, I bet," said Michael.

"Nope," his son said. "She's not."

"She's not?"

Alex shook his head. "One of the caterers has a question about pot holders, and I figured she'd be the one to answer."

Michael shrugged. "She was gone from the bed when I woke up," he said. "I assumed she was off running some last-minute errand or another."

"Yeah, that must be it," said Alex. "Well, I'll leave you to your moment of vanity, Dad. I never knew you had it in you."

Michael laughed, turning back to the mirror, yet even as he dismissed the idea of vanity, he knew that what his son said was true: He did feel a slight surge of something here—if not outright vanity, then at least confidence in how he looked. At age forty, Michael still had his hair, and though it wasn't as thick as it used to be, it was there. And he hadn't let himself start to go soft in the stomach as other men did in their forties; instead, he still played a strenuous if erratic game of tennis three times a week with his friend Jeff from the furniture workshop.

Alex closed the door gently behind him, and Michael returned to the task at hand. But ten minutes later, while he was polishing his second shoe, there came another knock on the door, and this time it was Rachel, saying that no one could find Mom and they were all getting concerned.

"All right," said Michael. "I'll come down in a minute."

Rachel left, and Michael put down the half-shined shoe and the soft piece of chamois. It was at that moment that something in him moved, lurched, gave a start. He felt his heart quicken and some kind of chemical begin to pour into his blood. He stood up suddenly, and for a moment, he caught a glimpse of himself in the full-length mirror, and this time what he saw disturbed him. It was amazing the way you could look at yourself one minute and like what you saw and then the next minute want to throw something at the glass. For now when he gazed at himself, he saw a ridiculous middle-aged man with one shoe. A man who looked tired and scared.

"Casey!" Michael called, and he flung open the bedroom door. "Casey!" he called again into the hallway, but the only voices he heard were the caterers', buzzing in the kitchen below. Michael systematically went from room to room, opening each door and finding the room empty, yet calling her name anyway, as if, by shouting it often enough, he could restore Casey's presence to the house.

Because by then he knew: His wife had left him.

Michael slumped down right where he was, on the wide, carpeted stairs. From where he was sitting, he could see her van out a window. It was still in the driveway, but that didn't mean anything, really, for she could have easily walked away from here. She could have walked to the train station, or the bus station, or even called a taxi to come and get her. She could have left the van there deliberately, to delay suspicion. Why hadn't he always known this might happen eventually? he asked himself. But the fact was, he told himself, he always had. That potential was part of who Casey was. He'd tried and he'd tried; he'd done whatever was in his power to do, but it still hadn't been enough to make Casey entirely happy—or entirely his, anyway.

Michael leaned weakly against a wooden post on the stairs. He was thinking of the day, so long ago, when he had shown up on the front door of this very house and asked Casey to come up to Providence with him. He wondered now whether it had really been a rescue, or perhaps something else. He'd always known that in some way it was partially an act of selfishness, that not only did he have to help her but he had to help himself, too. Up at college in Providence that fall, he had felt a loneliness so profound it made it impossible for him to concentrate. Call it the curse of a happy childhood, of having people around who loved you and a wonderful girl next door who was always there when you wanted her to be, but whatever it was, when he was on his own, he realized he was lost. At night, lying in his dormitory room with the sculpture student snorting and burbling in the bed across the way, Michael would fear for what might become of him.

He would lie in his own bed and imagine that he was holding Casey against him. All he wanted to do was to marry her, to claim her as his own, to be with her all the time. To know that no matter what else happened in life, this would endure: their time together. She might resist at first, he told himself back then, but in the long run she would see the wisdom of what he was talking about.

And now the long run was here. It was everywhere around him, wasn't it? A party that, like all the other sentimental touches he was always adding to every occasion, was designed to help him push away the truth.

Michael would forever remain a ridiculous man with one shoe on. He would forever think of this day, with the caterers arranging platters of food in the kitchen, and his three children flitting around the house like the most industrious hummingbirds on earth, and no one yet aware that the party was off. He should have seen it coming—not just over the years but recently, *last night*. There had been something in Casey's eyes last night; it was definitely there, and it scared him, so he hadn't mentioned it.

It scared him, so he hadn't mentioned it. Michael heard himself make a guttural sound, a low roar of disgust at himself. He leaned the side of his head into the wood of the post, hard, until his temple ached. If he were a stronger person, a braver man, he would have come home from work one afternoon years ago, taken her hand in his, and said, "Tell me what's missing."

The paintings on the walls that they'd bought at the roadside antique stores she loved to visit; the knickknacks; the little pieces of china and folk art from around the world, none of it worth much, but all of it distinctly theirs; the furniture he'd built—

God, the furniture he'd built with his own hands in his studio, loaded onto the back of a truck, hauled up the steps and into the places where his eye for design told him they belonged, as if he couldn't fill up the corners of the house fast enough: These were not missing from their life. These he could see, from the stairs, everywhere he looked. It hurt to look at them. He saw everything now, and it hurt his eyes, as though it was all made up of shards of unbearably bright light. It was too much to bear, he knew, and yet, somehow, it was not nearly enough to fill a marriage.

Casey had gotten up with the sun, rising from the bed in the dim orange light of the room. Michael was still asleep when she awoke, his face turned away from her, which somehow made it easier to leave. Down the hall, in their own bedrooms, the twins were sleeping, and so was Alex. They were a slumbering family, innocent, deep in dreams, these people she loved and had lived with. None of them heard her as she slipped into her jacket and scooped up her keys from the ceramic pot in the front hall. None of them heard her as she went out the front door and walked over to the Longwood Falls Inn. She wanted to walk, wanted to feel the air and stretch her legs and look around her at the town, in which she had spent almost her entire life.

Will, too, was asleep when she arrived. Opening the door of his suite, he smiled groggily and ushered her inside. "You're early," he murmured. "But I'm glad you are. Come to bed, love. Come lie with me before we have to go to the airport."

Casey looked over toward the large, rumpled bed in the middle of the room, which very recently had held his sleeping body. Will wore gray cotton pajamas, expensive ones, perhaps purchased by his wife at a good San Francisco department store. His hair was as rumpled as the bed, and the entire effect was one of vulnerability, as though he were not a forty-year-old, or a nineteen-year-old, but instead an eight-year-old, roused from bed too early. She noticed, again, the scar on his chin, and suddenly she realized what it was from, and who had put it there. She pictured Michael's raised arm, and the wrench flashing as it was swung.

"No," Casey said to him softly. "I won't lie down with you. But I do want to talk."

The Fountain

꒛

Will turned on one of the muted lamps in the room and then called room service to order coffee and breakfast pastries, though Casey insisted she wasn't remotely hungry. Then he pulled on a terry cloth robe, and they sat in the two easy chairs by the window of the suite's living room. It was strange; with her fully dressed and him in his pajamas and robe, there was an asymmetry between them, an imbalance of power. She'd never wanted power before, yet here it was.

"I can't go away with you," she told him.

Will blinked a few times, as though he hadn't heard her correctly. "You've gotten cold feet," he finally said. "That's understandable. It's a big change. A life change. And it will be very hard at first, I know that."

But Casey shook her head. "It isn't cold feet," she said. "It's something else. A cold heart, maybe. Or at least a practical one."

A waiter from room service knocked on the door then, and Will stood and opened it. Casey was glad for the momentary release from this difficult conversation, and she sat quietly while the waiter removed silver covers from plates of warm rolls and muffins and then poured coffee into china cups. When he was gone, the door clicking shut softly behind him, Casey continued what she had to say. "My father-in-law sat me down yesterday when I got home. And he told me everything, Will."

"Everything?" said Will, his spoon poised above his coffee cup. "I'm not sure what that means. You'll have to enlighten me."

"Everything about you and Dorian Bradley," she said.

For a long moment, Will said nothing. Then, finally, he put down his spoon, resting it on the saucer with a light clinking sound. "Ah," he said. "So. The great Dorian Bradley makes a reappearance, after all these years."

"Why didn't you tell me?" Casey said, her voice rising up into a shrill tone she didn't much like but couldn't prevent.

"I couldn't. I just had to leave," said Will. "Michael was right that night; I wasn't going to get over Dorian, at least not for a while. I'd remain obsessed, and I'd probably end up cheating on you. So I got the hell away from you instead. It was the moral thing to do."

The Fountain

❧

"I don't mean, why didn't you tell me back *then*?" said Casey. "I mean, why didn't you tell me yesterday? Yesterday, when we were at the boarding-house, and I asked you why you'd left. It was supposed to be our big moment of honesty, of coming clean to each other after all this time." She paused, then said, "You *lied* to me, Will. You lied to me back then and, even more important, you lied to me yesterday. How can I ever believe you again? How can I ever trust you? The answer is that I can't. You're someone who says whatever he wants people to believe. I mean, my God, is it even true that your wife Julie left you the other day just because things 'weren't working'? Or is there more to that story? Were you seeing another woman? Is that it? And if you're so lost, then why did you come to *me* after all this time instead of Dorian, wherever she is?"

"Dorian and I have nothing more to say to each other," Will said. "We already said everything."

"And what does that mean?"

"It means," he said wearily, "that when I left you the night before the wedding, I did wander around on my own for a while as I told you. But what I didn't tell you is that a few months later, Dorian came and joined me in San Francisco, after I left the fishing boat. We lived together briefly there. And we fought all the time, just like we used to. It was dreadful. She was afraid that one day I'd start looking at other women, and in a way it was a self-fulfilling prophecy, because sure enough I did start. And that was how I met my first wife, Cynthia. At a nightclub. So Dorian and I split up for good, and we agreed that though we loved each other—and were still obsessed with each other, really—we could never make a good couple."

"Where is she now?" Casey asked.

"She lives in Paris," he said. "Married to a French musician, a violinist in a symphony there. He's considerably older than she is, and when she wrote to me some years ago—the only time I've ever heard from her since we broke up—she told me that they have one daughter. Dorian runs a music school for children; it's quite successful. I got the general impression," he added stiffly, "that she's very happy."

"Good for her," said Casey softly. "I'm glad." She had no animosity toward Dorian, none at all, and was pleased to have solved the mystery of what had become of her. Casey still had plenty in common with Dorian, she realized. Like her old piano teacher, Casey now knew irrefutably that a life with Will Combray would never work.

"I have to go now," she said to him, looking out the hotel window and seeing that the day had grown bright and full, knowing that fairly soon her household on Strawberry Street would start to stir.

"That's it?" said Will, astonished. "You won't change your mind? Please, Casey, won't you reconsider?"

"No," she said. "I won't. I could have just not shown up this morning. I could have done exactly what you did, all those years ago. Jilted you. But I didn't want to do that to you. Instead, I wanted to explain."

Yet there was something that she didn't want to explain to him, something that she wanted to keep entirely to herself. It was what she had realized last night, lying in bed beside Michael and trying to make sense of everything that had happened at the boardinghouse that afternoon, everything that Tom had told her. She realized that she'd always underestimated Michael. Good, solid Michael, as sturdy and handsome as one of his pieces of furniture. She'd always seen him as long-suffering and infinitely patient, and she had loved him for it. He was a man who could put up with more things than she would have ever thought possible. He'd stayed awake with the children when they were babies, walking them around and around the yard, just as his own father had done a generation earlier. He'd spent so many hours in his furniture studio, trying to get the curve of a rocking chair's arm exactly the way he wanted it, not a degree off. And he'd stayed with her all these years, knowing that if she'd had her way long ago, she would have been somewhere else. Patient, faithful Michael, that was how she'd seen him.

But suddenly, after hearing Tom Becket's story, she was seeing another view: Michael in Dorian Bradley's house, furious and chivalrous and swinging a wrench, Michael who had behaved swiftly and violently in a way that was frightening and shocking, yes, but also in a way that had made his feelings impossible to miss. *I swear to God, I won't let you hurt her*, he'd said, and he'd meant it with all his heart.

I'm so sorry, Michael, Casey had thought this morning at dawn as she watched her husband sleep. She'd had the desire to wake him up and tell him everything she'd found out; she suddenly wanted to kiss his neck and his mouth and feel the long strength of him in a way she hadn't done in quite some time. In a way that perhaps she'd never done, for which she was sorry—sorrier than she could possibly say.

But none of this could she tell to Will. For it was private, it was part of her marriage to Michael, and she did not want to dishonor her husband in this way.

She stood now in the hotel room and walked over to Will. Very lightly, she reached out and touched the scar on his chin, feeling the smoothness there, which would never go away. She let Will hold her briefly against him, and she could feel his heart thudding somewhere beneath the warm folds of his robe. What if she had gone away with him, as she'd planned? What if, what if? There were some questions that could never be answered, and other questions that *should* never be answered, and this one was both.

Will walked her to the door of the suite, and for one fleeting moment before she left, she caught a glimpse of the nineteen-year-old he'd once been, his smile crooked and irresistible and plaintive all at once. *Enough*, Casey thought, and then she turned and walked out into the brightening day.

Michael sat on the steps of the house for a long time. He was paralyzed there, unable to stand up and tell the children what it was that had happened. *Your mother is gone*, he would say. No. *Mom has left.* No, not quite right. *Mom has left me.* All of these versions were unbearable to imagine, and somehow, if he said one of them aloud, it would magically come true. Whereas, if he simply sat here forever on the stairs, then perhaps it wouldn't. He could remain here like Rip Van Winkle, sleeping his life away, keeping the painful truth at bay.

"Michael?" came a voice suddenly, interrupting this mournful stream of thought. His head jerked up. Someone was calling him from far, far away, almost as though from another world. "Michael?"

"Casey!" he called back, springing to a standing position. "Casey!"

She was here, after all; but where? Where? He needed to know right this minute. Her voice sounded so distant. Michael held his breath, thrilled that she was here, that he had overreacted, that he had been wrong, that she hadn't left at all. Yet where, literally, was she?

"I'm up here!" Casey cried.

"Up where?" he called, climbing blindly, stumbling, righting himself, charging on. "Up where?"

"In the attic!" she called to him.

They never used the attic; what in the world was she doing up there? "Only madwomen belong in attics," he'd once said to her, many years ago, when she'd suggested that they could turn the attic into a wonderful playroom for the children.

"I almost became a madwoman," she'd replied, referring to the year Will had left and then her parents had been killed.

"Hardly," he'd said. "You came through okay in the end."

"Only because of you," Casey said, but Michael shook his head.

"No, because of you," he told her. "Because of who you were, who you are. It wasn't me, Casey. Or, at least, maybe it was partly me, but mostly it was you. Sorry to spoil the illusion, but you were never destined to become a madwoman."

The attic, as it would turn out, had been a less

than ideal space for a playroom, given how it trapped all the heat from the house in the warmer months, and so Casey and Michael never really did anything with it. Instead, it remained purely a storage place for old furniture, toys, and clothes, and Michael couldn't imagine what Casey was doing all the way up there on the morning of their anniversary party, when she was so clearly needed downstairs. But he didn't really care, so relieved was he with the idea that he hadn't lost her after all. He loped down the hall toward the back stairs. Then he reached up to the little square inlaid into the ceiling that contained the ladder to the attic, and he pulled open the latch and let the ladder drop down. For some reason, Casey had closed the hatch after her, as though she hadn't wanted anyone to know she was there. He climbed carefully now, slowly, his heart racing all the while, and in a moment he hoisted himself up by his arms into the attic.

The room was broiling, insufferable. He looked around him at the network of cobwebs and the dust swirling in beams of light and the hulking figures of old, unloved furniture.

"Casey?" he said.

And then she appeared, coming out from behind a chest of drawers that used to stand in the front hall, back when her parents owned the house.

And he saw, in that moment, that she was wearing her wedding dress.

It was the dress she'd been wearing the day she was to marry Will Combray. He'd never forgotten the way Casey had looked in that dress, when he'd peered out the side window of his house before the ceremony and briefly saw her in her own window next door, the shade flung up, dressed for the day and waiting. A bridesmaid had helped her with her veil and then stood back to look at her. And Michael, for one moment, had looked, too. Seeing her had taken his breath away then, and took it away now. He stared dumbly at her, wondering if she could still see the leftover fear in his eyes, and how it had been so recently replaced with wild relief and then, right now, with emotion.

"Michael," she said softly, after a moment, "where's your other shoe?"

By the time Casey had returned home from the Longwood Falls Inn early that morning, her family was still asleep. She had just been through an intense, dreamlike drama with Will, and now she longed to be done with it, to get back to the business of the day: the anniversary party. It was then that she remembered her pale blue dress, which she had neglected to pick up from the cleaner's yesterday, after she and Will had been to the boardinghouse. Here she was, going to her own twentieth anniversary party, and she had nothing to wear, Casey realized.

It was then that something occurred to her. Of course, she told herself, and she walked to the back stairs and pulled down the attic ladder. Up she went into the place that she seldom entered, so unpleasantly airless and dusty was it. But this morning she barely felt the heat as she walked across the floorboards toward the armoire all the way at the back of the long, slope-ceilinged space.

Carefully, Casey pulled open the doors, and there it was, wrapped in plastic and carefully preserved over all these years: her wedding dress. She hadn't seen it since her daughters had found it about six years earlier, but even then she had made sure the dress was quickly returned to its armoire, because she hadn't wanted the spell to be broken. The spell of Will.

Now that spell was broken. Now she was in the attic, gently removing her wedding dress from its protective covering and holding it up to examine it closely. Would it do? Yes, yes it would. The dress was as delicate and beautiful as it had been the day she'd gone with her mother to buy it at Albany Traditional Bridal. But the more relevant question, of course, was, would it fit?

Casey stepped out of her nightgown and awkwardly stepped into the dress. The last time she had tried it on, she'd had a ring of bridesmaids to help her. Today she was over twenty years older and all alone, yet still she managed to put it on, and to her surprise and pleasure she found that the dress still fit. She had remained small and narrow-bodied all her life, despite giving birth to three children; it was a combination of good genes and being careful about what she ate, and all of it somehow conspired to make the wedding dress slip onto her with relative ease. Her hand trembling, Casey buttoned the row of seed-pearl buttons. Then she smoothed down the front and fluffed up the skirt with both hands. Ideally, the dress would have been pressed and starched and given a good readying for the party, but there obviously wasn't going to be time for that. Still, it looked fine, Casey thought as she turned one way, then the other, in front of the dusty oval mirror.

This dress—the dress she'd chosen to marry Will in—was the dress she should have worn the day she'd married Michael. Had she done that, it would have showed a depth of feeling for him that such a dress implied. But she'd married him because he was someone she loved and trusted, and because he'd asked her to, and because she thought otherwise she might go mad. She'd been grateful, and it was with that in mind that she'd picked out an understated, ordinary skirt and blouse: gratitude. A wedding dress, however, was for romance, and a deep and abiding passion.

Which was why she was wearing it today.

Casey wasn't sure how long she'd been up in the attic when she realized that a voice was calling her from somewhere down below. She called back, and eventually Michael found her. She wasn't ready for him to see her; she had wanted to surprise him. But it was all right. Michael's head popped up from the hole in the floor, and he searched the room for her. After a moment, Casey came out from behind the chest of drawers and let him see her, hoping that what he saw would be good enough.

First she made a joke about his shoe being missing, but he ignored it. "Look at you," he said in reply, entering the attic. "Look at you."

Michael walked across the room and came right up to her. He looked and looked, and she just let him do that for a while. He walked around her in a slow circle, his hand lightly touching the material. When he had completed one full revolution and faced her again, she saw that his eyes were flooding with tears.

"I almost lost you, didn't I?" he asked her, and she hesitated just a moment before she nodded, and then she began crying, too. "But you're back," he said.

She nodded, standing still, helpless, her arms at her sides, sobbing openly now.

"For good?"

Without saying anything, Casey walked into his arms and stayed there. He didn't even ask why he had almost lost her or why, in the end, she hadn't gone; that was the kind of man he was. It wasn't a lack of curiosity or a fear of knowing the truth. It was simply that the specific reasons didn't matter. She was back for good; that much he knew, and that was enough. He would have no way of knowing that Will Combray had entered their backyard two days ago, or that his father had broken his promise and told her what had happened the night before she was supposed to have married Will.

No, Michael wasn't intuitive the way Will was. He wouldn't be able to look at a business prospectus and decide whether it would succeed or fail, and he didn't have an instinct about people the way Will did. Yet Michael had recognized the truth about Will that night at Dorian's. Had recognized it, had known what to do about it, had done it. He had made Will see the truth, too, which then sent Will off on his motorcycle, out of Casey's life for over two decades.

"I can't believe how you look," Michael said, trying to smooth down the fabric of the dress.

"Don't worry," she assured him, "it's already creased. It's been hanging here in this attic for over two decades without being touched by an iron. I think it can tolerate your touch."

So he touched. Michael touched her and kissed her more fully now, feeling the warmth of her mouth against his, and they could have stayed in the heat of the attic for a long, long time, except for the fact that soon they heard the voice of their son, calling their names with increasing alarm, just as Michael had earlier gone searching for Casey.

"The guests are probably arriving," Michael said in a slight daze.

Casey peered out the small, diamond-shaped window. "Yes," she said, "they are."

From all the way up here, she could see the line of cars arriving on Strawberry Street, and the men and women crossing the lawns toward the house, dressed for the occasion, carrying the gifts they had been specifically instructed *not* to bring. Michael stood beside her, both of them watching everyone arrive from this safe remove.

"I guess we should go down," he said, and together they walked across the attic floor, and he helped her down the ladder in her dress. Their faces were flushed from all the heat and the crying and the kissing. Their hair was slightly wild, too, as though they were two teenagers who had just emerged from the shadows.

Suddenly, Rachel was there on the back stairs. "Mom?" she said, astonished. "You're in your—I mean, look at you. The wedding dress!" She shrieked once and ran her hand along the fabric. "God, you guys," she went on. "This is so romantic!"

"Yes, it is," Casey said, thinking that was just the word for it, the word that Dorian Bradley had long ago said united her with Casey.

"Cool!" Hannah said now, hurrying down the hall toward them. "That is so . . . cool!" She fingered a sleeve, then stepped back to admire the whole effect. "God," she said to her father, "it must bring back a ton of memories to see Mom in this dress again."

"Oh, it certainly does," said Michael mildly.

He and Casey didn't dare look at each other for fear that they might start to laugh. The twins looked back and forth from one face to the other, probably wondering what the joke was and what in the world was going on between their parents.

The Fountain

"Shall we?" Casey said, turning to Michael. "Everyone's waiting."

Michael took her by the arm, and they descended the stairs together, then walked through the kitchen and out onto the back steps. There, they stopped and surveyed their world.

The yard was filled with people they had known throughout the years: friends from school and from the furniture studio and from the neighborhood. Some of their children's old friends were there, too, and the parents of those friends: a whole, complete universe of people, the kind that populated any married couple's life over time. There were the Danforths from around the corner, and the Mitchells and the Bestons, and there was Alex entwined with his girlfriend, Amy, the two of them looking for all the world like one organism. When Michael and Casey arrived, he in his suit, she beside him in her wedding dress, some of those guests called out their congratulations. Someone was taking pictures, the camera whirring as it went quickly from frame to frame. Over at the side of the lawn, standing by the patch of zinnias, stood Tom and Janice Becket. Casey couldn't be sure, but she thought that Tom nodded to her; it was almost a bow. If her own mother and father could somehow be here now after all these years, Casey thought—and she so deeply wished they could—how surprised they would be to see Michael and Casey joined together. Astonished, really.

Yet no less astonished than she was at this moment. Standing here at the top of the steps, she and Michael would appear to everyone gathered before them to belong to each other in a way that everyone had probably assumed they always had. But it was only now, as the music played and the guests raised their glasses, and as the two stone angels in the fountain looked on, that Michael Becket—for the first time, and at long last—led his bride out onto the lawn.

Rita Award-winning author

Georgia Bockoven

"Bockoven is magic."
New York Times bestselling author Catherine Coulter

ANOTHER SUMMER
0-380-81865-5/$6.99 US/$9.99 Can
"*Another Summer* is Georgia Bockoven at her very best.
Heartbreaking and uplifting, poignant and triumphant . .
it will appeal to anyone who believes
in the healing power of love."
Kristin Hannah

Also by the author

THE BEACH HOUSE
0-06-108440-9/$6.50 US/$8.50 Can

DISGUISED BLESSING
0-06-103020-1/$6.50 US/$8.99 Can